Conly, Jane Leslie

TROUT SUMMER

DATE DUE

Trout Summer

Trout Summer

Jane Leslie Conly

Henry Holt and Company
New York

Henry Holt and Company, Inc.
Publishers since 1866
115 West 18th Street
New York, New York 10011

Henry Holt is a registered
trademark of Henry Holt and Company, Inc.

Published in Canada by Fitzhenry & Whiteside Ltd.,
195 Allstate Parkway, Markham, Ontario L3R 4T8.

Library of Congress Cataloging-in-Publication Data
Conly, Jane Leslie.
Trout summer / Jane Leslie Conly.
p.   cm.
Summary: A sister and brother spend a largely unsupervised summer
in a cabin near a river, where they befriend an elderly man with
much to teach them and where they try to come to terms with their
parents' failing marriage and make decisions about their own
futures.
[1. Brothers and sisters—Fiction.   2. Old age—Fiction.
3. Rivers—Fiction.   4. Canoes and canoeing—Fiction.
5. Summer—Fiction.]   I. Title.
PZ7.C761846Tr   1995
[Fic]—dc20   95-16381

ISBN 0-8050-3933-3
First Edition—1995
Printed in the United States of America
on acid-free paper.∞
1 3 5 7 9 10 8 6 4 2

For Paul, Mischa, and Sam—
may adventures and poetry fill your days.

Trout Summer

One

---

*I'm waiting for Cody to come back. He's gone for the canoe
so we can try to save the life of this old man, the one who's
lying here on the riverbank by my feet with a great big puddle
of blood around his head and his heart beating so fast it
could give out any second. We thought we knew who he was,
but it turned out we were wrong, that he's a damn crazy
liar just like a lot of other people we know. But we can't
watch him bleed to death, Cody says, so we're taking the
boat toward the rapids: Dog's Breath and Horseshoe, Deerfoot and Blindman's Falls, where somebody died last spring.
If we make it through, there are summer cabins on the other
side. Somebody there will have a telephone.*

*I wipe the blood from the old man's head and I say my
prayers: God, if there is a God, help us make it down the
river. I'll do whatever you want from now on. And if there's
any good to spare, could you save the old man, too?*

Two

---

*T*hat's over now, but it's not where the story begins. I don't know if it starts when we found the cabin, or when Mama and Cody and I moved to Laglade, or when Daddy met the new waitress at the Peter Pan Inn, or even before that: twelve years ago, when Cody was born, or when I, Shana, was born thirteen years ago; or when Mama and Daddy met in the parking lot of the Super-fresh Market in Warrensburg, Virginia, where he was selling a stringer of bass he'd caught that afternoon in the Castle River. I guess the best way to explain is like what Cody and I do when we're standing hot and sweaty on the riverbank: plunge in.

How would you feel if the members of your family were like dice and somebody stuck you in a shaker and tossed you around and threw you out any old way? The first time, you might land together in a heap, but the next throw would send the Dad dice flying off the table for a couple of months, and the one after that would sling someone else out of the way, once and for all. Over time the dice would get fewer, the shakes harder. Just as you thought you were used to it, you'd get swooped up and flung around again, knocking against people and places and feelings as if that's what they were meant for: to hurt you. If it happened to you enough, you might turn out like me: dreaming about a happy, smiling family like you see on television; holding in your hands the scraps from a family picture torn up because there was no family left.

My daddy was a big smiler. I've got pictures of him on the wall of my bedroom in the Laglade townhouse: Daddy on ice skates; in a cowboy hat and boots on top of Mr. Roy's horse, Dinah; sipping coffee with the regulars at the Peter Pan Inn, studying his book of Italian art. That picture ran in the Warrensburg paper last fall, in an article about the men who drop by the restaurant to talk about politics and weather, fertilizer and fish bait. The article allowed as how Daddy, with his interest in Leonardo and Raphael, was an oddball there. But we were proud of the picture. It was pinned on the cupboard door in the kitchen of the old house for a good long time.

Up until Easter, I'd lived in that house all my life. It

belonged to Mama's daddy, who lived with us till I was seven. Then cancer killed him. That was one of those shakes of the dice that sent me reeling, because somebody I loved every single day got carried away in an ambulance and never came back.

The house: It was white clapboard on the outside, faded and off-color like shingles get, with a big front porch and a little back porch and the Castle River running right through the back field, so you could look down anytime, day or night, and see the water. The rooms were small: the front room with an old black oil-burning stove and faded wallpaper; the kitchen with the hand pump still there, even though there'd been running water since Mama was a teenager; and lots of windows, and the vegetable garden right out behind where you could see if the weeds were starting to take over. On the left was Mama and Daddy's bedroom, with Daddy's notebooks lying here and there on the wooden bookshelves he'd made, and the big iron bed where Cody and I would bounce if they went out. Granddaddy's room was beside Mama and Daddy's. After he died, they moved the TV and a sofa bed in there, because the oil stove in the front room can be smelly when you first light it. Upstairs was my room, small and tucked under the back eaves, where I could see the river. Cody's was in the front, looking out on the lilacs with the road and the town just beyond.

It hurts to leave the place that's raised you. Losing

people is bad enough, although until they're dead, like Granddaddy, you dream you'll get them back. But the land will show you all its secrets, if you look. I must have known—still do—every little hollow in the ground that led down to the river, every gully or washed-out spot where a kid could curl up to hide or read or spy on someone else. I knew the clearings in the middle of the blackberry bushes, the space between tree trunks where I'd tried over the years to build lean-tos and playhouses. I knew—know—where the spring rises up, and how the ground smells just before you get there, that damp cool smell of wet earth, wet stone. I've lain on my stomach and seen the sun shine off the spring water, seen the moon and stars like the spring was a cup that held them, and you could put your face down in the darkness and swallow them up.

Most of all, better than I knew the house or maybe even the land out back, I knew the river. My memory begins there: sitting beside Daddy on the bank, clutching a bamboo pole, him saying to me, "Shana! Pull *now*!" I did, and up came a fish with blue and gold along her underside, wiggling to get back where she came from. I didn't want to kill her, so Daddy ran up to the house and got a bucket, and we filled it with water and carried her up and showed Granddaddy and Mama and Cody.

"You shouldn't have left Shana down there by herself while you got the bucket," Mama fussed. "What if she fell in?"

"She didn't fall in," Daddy said. "I knew she wouldn't."

"I'm naming her Fairy," I told them. I wanted to keep her in the bucket overnight, but they said she would die, so all of us took her down to the river and let her go.

I didn't free all my fish, not after I tasted what they were like rolled in cornmeal and fried up beside a couple of eggs, with potatoes on the side. I must have fed the family lots of those breakfasts, because after I caught Fairy I had Granddaddy take me down to the river almost every day to fish. We'd troop down together, him and Cody and me, because Mama'd already got her job as a telephone operator, and Daddy was either working or studying or looking for work. I got to know the river in all its seasons and all its times: morning, when the mist rose off it like magic breath; midday, with the dragonflies hovering and swirling and the muskrats leaving their water trails beside the banks; evening, when the deer came out of the woods on the other side to drink and spy on us two-legged ones before they turned tail-up and ran. Late at night we took our flashlights down and fished catfish on the bottom. That's Mama's favorite, because it's sweet, like chicken. Served up beside ripe tomatoes from the garden with a glass of ice tea, it makes a meal you can't buy at the Peter Pan.

Cody and I must have pulled hundreds of fish out of

the Castle: bluegills and perch, red-eyes and cats, willow bass and black bass. These last we caught mostly on lures: rubber worms, spinners, flatfish. We learned to fish the deep spots where the water stays cool even in July for largemouth, and to cast across the cobble bars, in and out of pools, for willow bass.

We didn't always catch fish. Some days we'd have everything perfect: the right bait, a good lunch in the backpack, a pair of old sneakers tied to our belts for wading the rocky shallows. As the hours passed, we thought our luck was bound to change with the next cast or around the bend. "There's a great place just behind that rock," Cody would say, not adding that you'd have to be an Olympic swimmer to reach it. Cody can pick the spots, I'll hand him that. As crazy as he is, he'll risk his life to get there, too.

What Cody lacked—and this balanced us out as a team—was patience. A snarl in his line would start him cussing so loud you'd hear him all the way across the river. Later he'd show up beside me, in tears from exasperation, his rod in his hand. Usually I can pick out a tangle, but sometimes I'd take my time before I agreed to do it. "Will you let me watch what I want on TV tonight?"

"Shana!" His eyes would turn dark, and he'd cross his arms and stare out over the water. Now and then he grabbed my bait and ran. Sometimes he did promise. Once the reel was working, he'd stalk off without saying thank you. But he stuck to his bargains, and he often caught a good one, to boot.

But he let his go. Cody's softhearted, though he tries to hide it. If he thought the fish was going to die anyway, he'd put it on the stringer, but he wouldn't look at it, after that; he said it made him feel bad, seeing it hurt and knowing he was the reason why. It didn't bother me. I told him, somebody kills all our meat. He didn't like that, and he said when he got older and cooked for himself, he planned to be a vegetarian.

The river wasn't just for fishing. Cody and I must have had a dozen places that were special to us: the rock we'd jump off where the current would swirl us around the bend on our way up; the place with the sand beach; the spot where sycamores grew out over the water, where we strung the swinging rope and the town kids would come watch us and ask: "Can I try it?" That was the only thing they ever envied us for, and we got what we could from it, making them share their Coke and chips before we'd climb up and unwind the rope from the high branches. Though they lived nearby, they didn't know the river like we did. You'd hear one of them say, "Look at that red flower. Ain't that pretty?"

"Cardinal flower," Cody would murmur to me, or "Bluebells," or "Trout lily." Granddaddy had taught us the trees and flowers, just like he'd taught Mama when she was little.

Daddy loved the river too. He grew up fishing and skating and swimming on the other side of Warrensburg. He went to high school at the regional. People said he was the smartest boy that school ever had. He qualified for the quiz show *I've Got a Question*, and they flew him to New York for an interview, but they didn't let him on because he had bad teeth. If he'd gotten on, he would have been the youngest contestant the show ever had.

Daddy was interested in art back then, too. He took every class the high school offered. But he didn't have the money to go to college, so he had to study on his own. He also loved to ice skate. He taught himself to do some of those fancy jumps you see on TV. And when I was born, he named me after his favorite skater: Shana LaPont. He watched her in the World Championships and the Olympics on TV, and when she came to Richmond to give an exhibition, he went to see her there, and took me, too. I can't remember it, but he said she made a fuss over me. Cody says she was probably faking, since I was bald and fat; but who knows?

By the time Cody was born, Daddy's interests had changed. He was doing long-distance trucking with a partner named Mel, and they'd made a pact to drive in every state in the Union. Daddy took pictures of them all. I loved to sit beside him and look at them: the red sands of New Mexico, the Chesapeake Bay country, the forests of the Ozarks in Missouri. He said one day he'd put them in a book and get it published. He'd been in twenty-two states when he passed through Wyoming and saw a rodeo. He named Cody after the town where he saw it, and for years after that he was desperate to get a horse. I was wild with hope that he would, but Mama put a lid on it, saying, "We can hardly afford the car, much less a horse."

"A horse doesn't cost that much. I'd fence the back field and it could feed on grass right up to the end of November. Save us having to cut back there."

"What about winter?" Mama was smiling, but she looked skeptical.

"It doesn't take much to feed a horse, honey. Twenty, thirty bales of hay. I could get that off Roy Haines. Hell, I could work for it, earn it in a weekend."

"Yes, yes!" I cried. I was running around in circles, dizzy with joy.

"You've got a job already," Mama said.

"I'm sick of it, Dot. I'm away from home, away from you and the kids, and it makes me lonely. And there's no excitement to it anymore, no romance." He paused. "I was thinking of putting my name in for work at the livestock market in Hopewell. In the meantime, if I have to, I'll work at the cement plant at Grove Hill."

Mama sighed. "Charlie, they're laying off down there."

"There's other places. Mel and I don't get along like we used to, and he drinks too much. And Cody's nearly three. I've missed seeing him grow. I want to stay home awhile."

"And get a horse!" I shouted.

Mama gave me a look that said be quiet.

"Money isn't everything," Daddy said.

"I thought you wanted to finish out your fifty states," Mama said. "You're just nine shy of the whole country."

"They're not going anywhere. When the kids are older, we'll take a trip and see them all."

He did what he wanted to. Not that Mama didn't like her job. She worked every week and every other weekend, and she got good pay. On Fridays we'd put her check in the bank and go to the supermarket, and if anybody needed something big like shoes or a coat, we'd buy it then, while Mama had the money in her account. Granddaddy's Social Security went for heating oil, or to repair the house if it was something he couldn't do himself. Daddy's money was used for emergencies or special times: birthdays and Christmas. Daddy loved holidays. He made sure the space under the tree was jammed with presents. The year I turned five, I remember coming down the stairs Christmas morning and seeing pink: dollhouse and snowsuit and stuffed animals and a brand-new pink two-wheeler. That day I must have been the happiest kid on earth.

Cody was born too late for the best times. He'd just turned six when Granddaddy died. He started first grade a month later, and he had to go to old Mrs. Reese for day care in the afternoons. Mama was worried about Cody, about all of us. Daddy was away a lot, looking for work. He'd call to say he'd be home Monday, but something would come up, and lots of times he wouldn't make it back till the weekend. I couldn't shut up about Granddaddy: Why did he die? Who gave him cancer? Why didn't the doctors have pills that would make him better?

Cody was just the opposite. When he wasn't in school, he stood at the window, looking out silently. I tried telling him what the grown-ups had told me: that Granddaddy was gone forever, that he was living some-place in the sky. Cody looked at me like I was nuts. "The sky is for birds," he said.

"Granddaddy isn't coming back," I repeated.

"He will, too," Cody said.

I wonder if that's where Cody lost his patience, be-cause he stood waiting at that window for close to a year before he finally gave up. By then he'd turned into a nervous, fidgety kid who had a hard time sitting still or staying out of fights at school. Even at home, when he'd sit down to watch TV or read, he'd wriggle and squirm, as if there was something inside that wouldn't leave him alone.

But Cody always had friends, boys who laughed at his high jinks and called good-bye out the windows of the school bus. I was a loner. I didn't dislike the other kids; I just couldn't think of anything to say, and the more I tried, the more tongue-tied I got, until after a while I stopped trying. It was easier to live inside the books I read. I talked with Nancy Drew about her latest mystery, and rode Misty and Sea Star over the dunes at Chincoteague. Sometimes I read stories to Cody so that we could act them out. As he got older he liked being read to, especially books about animals, like *The Incredible Journey* and *Rascal*.

By then Daddy had taken a job at the sawmill at Landis. He hated that work, but Mama said he was lucky to get it, the way the economy was slumping. In the long run it may have been the steadiest job he ever had, because Uncle Mike worked there too, and he tried to keep Daddy going. They got into the habit of stopping at the Peter Pan for coffee and sweets on the way to the mill. Everybody liked Uncle Mike; he was big and loud and jolly, and the waitresses hurried to fill his cup and give him the biggest slice of pie. Daddy was quiet by comparison. I've wondered who it was that said, "Charlie, this is Paula Preston. She's an art student at the university, taking time off to save money 'cause she wants to go to Europe."

"Europe!" Uncle Mike probably roared. "What for?"

Maybe she was too shy to answer him. Maybe Daddy asked her later, quietly, and she talked to him about Michelangelo and Leonardo and Giotto and Raphael. All I know for sure is that summer Daddy started taking me to the Peter Pan for breakfast Saturday mornings. He said it was to make up for the Tuesday nights he spent with Cody at baseball, though I hadn't minded having Cody out of the house so I could pick my own TV shows or read in peace. Sometimes Mama and I talked. She told me about her friends at work, who were forever entering contests and sweepstakes. "Why don't you try too?" I asked. "We might win a new car or a trip to Hawaii. It only costs a stamp."

She shrugged. Her dark hair was coming free from the neat coil she fixed each morning. "I know I won't win."

"How come?"

"I've never won anything in my life, Shana. I had to struggle for what I got." She smiled. "Except for you and Cody, that is."

"The more you don't win, the better the chances that you will next time, Mama."

"You can't rely on luck."

"I want a Hawaiian vacation. . . ."

"Your grass skirt is on layaway. If you get lucky, I might have it paid off by Christmas." Mama brushed my straight brown hair back from my face. I snuggled into the pillows of the old sofa, its blue afghan warm around my shoulders. The comfortable buzz of the TV lulled me to sleep.

• • •

The waitress at the Peter Pan had blue eyes, and when she looked at you, you could tell she was *really* looking. I turned red when Daddy explained I'd been named for a figure skater, but she had an easy laugh that made embarrassing moments slip away.

"You should eat, honey," she said, as if she wanted to fill out my skinny arms and legs. "How about a pile of flapjacks?"

I nodded, but when she brought them I was still so flustered it was hard to swallow.

"Paula's only working at the Peter Pan a little while," Daddy explained on the way home. "She's saving her money to go visit the Sistine Chapel."

"What's that?"

"It's a church in Rome, Italy. Some of the world's greatest art is on the walls and ceilings there."

"I think I've heard of it."

Daddy nodded, as if he were sure I'd heard of it. "Paula showed me some pictures she keeps in her handbag. They're breathtaking."

"It'll take her a long time to save money working at the Peter Pan," I said.

Daddy looked at me with surprise. "You sound like your mama."

For the next month Daddy couldn't stop talking about Italy, and the artists who'd lived there in the 1500s. He took a day off work and went to the library to check out a stack of books on Renaissance art. He'd thumb through them in the mornings before Uncle Mike came to pick him up, showing us the paintings and sculpture he liked best. That got on Cody's nerves. He'd roll his eyes when Daddy wasn't looking, and once, down by the river, he said, "Do you realize we're named after Daddy's hobbies?" Before I could answer, he added, "If Mama got pregnant now, they'd call the baby Leonardo."

"Cody! You know Mama and Daddy aren't going to have more children."

He looked taken aback. "Why not?"

I had to stop and think. It wasn't anything I'd heard them say that made me so sure I was right. "They're too old. They hardly even kiss anymore. Anyway, we can't afford another child."

"We could if they wanted it. Daddy hasn't worked a full week this month. He stays home writing in those dumb notebooks."

"They're not dumb."

"They are too. Shana, those people he's studying have been dead four hundred years! They're not important now."

"They are to him."

"He needs to get his head examined."

"Cody, you're mean."

He shrugged his thin shoulders. "So what?"

• • •

18

But when Daddy left before Easter, Cody was as upset as Mama and me. The note we found in the mailbox didn't tell us what we needed to know. I read the phrases over and over, as if they were pieces of a puzzle that would make sense if you got them in the right order: ". . . sorry to disappoint . . . time to study what I crave and figure out who I am . . . know that I have let you down . . ."

"It doesn't say where he's gone, or when he's coming back," I told Cody.

He shook his head. "He's dumping us like we're some boring TV show."

"Don't say that!"

"We should call Uncle Mike."

"Mama already did."

"What did he say?"

"He was shocked."

"This can't be true," I said, reading the note one more time.

"It is." Cody sounded tough, but I knew he was hurting too.

"Daddy's gone away before, when he was trucking or looking for work," I said finally. "He always came back, and he will again. It's just a matter of time."

Three

*E*verybody in Warrensburg heard about Daddy's leaving. We couldn't go anyplace without someone asking how we were doing or what we needed. Couples had broken up before, and some had gotten back together, but not before the town had the chance to hash over their problems. Now they couldn't stop putting Daddy down.

"I knew it would be hard for Charlie when he lost the chance to be a TV star," Mrs. Martin said, shoving our loaves of bread into a paper bag. "But I never thought he'd do you and the children like this. You asked so little. Why, that house came from your own daddy, didn't it, Dot? Charlie didn't have to pay a cent for it."

"Daddy offered us the house," Mama said. "He didn't like living alone."

"Charlie thought he was better than the rest of us," Mrs. Martin sniffed.

"That's why I married him," Mama said. She paid for the bread and let the screen door slam behind her.

When Mama brought up moving, it never occurred to any of us it would be permanent. I guess we thought we'd go someplace till the gossip died down and we could pull ourselves together. We'd never been anywhere except camping in the state parks, so the idea of seeing another state was inviting, a little vacation we'd stay on until Daddy came back to his senses and found us there. Then we'd return to Warrensburg together, walking down Main Street and stopping at the Peter Pan for hot chocolate and pie.

But Cody didn't want to leave. He told Mama, "Baseball's about to start. I'm supposed to pitch this year."

"Every place has baseball, Cody."

"But I know the hitters. I studied them last spring, to see what they swung at and where I'd have to keep the ball."

"Maybe you ought to wait a little while, Dot," Uncle Mike said. "Give the kids a chance to adjust to this before they have to make another change."

Mama shook her head wearily. "This town has such a hold on me. Ever since I was little, I've wanted to try something different. All the years Charlie traveled, he said we would. I was supposed to hold the fort until he had it figured out. We used to sit at night and look at his photographs: Florida would be nice, right between the bay and the ocean, but there's nothing like the Rockies. . . ." Mama's voice was worn out.

"Where would you go?"

"The phone company can transfer me. There's a pay increase when you move to a metropolitan area, and one suburb that needs operators has inexpensive town houses, too. I can rent this place out for extra money."

"Rent our house!" My eyes flew open, but Mama stayed calm.

"We wouldn't want it standing empty, Shana."

"There's worse places than Warrensburg," Uncle Mike said quietly.

"We'll be back," Mama said.

I was still in a daze when I first saw Laglade, Maryland. It looked like a picture from a magazine: row after row of pastel town homes, neat and clean, the grass cut and little trees planted every twenty feet beside the white sidewalks. The realtor who unlocked the door to our house and ushered us in must have guessed we were from the sticks, because she showed us the dishwasher and the sliding glass doors and the tiny back porch, which she called a deck. "The pool opens June first," she said. "And there are three malls within a ten-minute drive. King's Crossing has an A&P, and Havilland has a couple grocery stores too."

"We'll put things away and go stock up," Mama said cheerfully. "And tomorrow morning we'll get you registered at school."

Cody hated Laglade right from the get-go; maybe he would have hated anyplace, angry as he was then. But his complaints were right: Laglade was designed not for people but for cars. The sidewalks ended with the last town house, and after that came a snarl of expressways. He couldn't even get to a baseball diamond on foot.

The kids were different too. They all had Nintendo, and skateboarding was the in thing instead of baseball. They wore expensive sneakers and soccer shorts and cut their hair like bangs across the back. They weren't mean to us; they just didn't notice us at all. Cody made a fool of himself trying to get their attention. He borrowed a skateboard and rode it down a concrete drainage ditch until he crashed and had to get four stitches above his eye. He got into a fight on the playground, and he refused to do his homework because they did math a different way from how we'd been taught. Mama went through everything from begging to screaming. She hardly had time to ask how it was for me.

I'm not sure I could have answered her anyway. I was knocked dizzy by the latest tumble of the dice. Was Laglade ugly or beautiful? Did I like living in a house that looked like a picture in a magazine? Which of the girls at school liked to read and fish and swim, like me? A few of them giggled at my accent, but there were others that turned to shush them when they did. The kids didn't just repeat answers from the book, either— they spoke up about their ideas. One girl, called Catherine, wrote poetry so good that the teacher read it to the class. Mr. Thomas liked my writing too.

"You have talent, Shana," he said. "You should practice over the summer—keep a journal, and maybe try some poems. And when you get to high school, show them to Mrs. Kless. She teaches creative writing. Usually you have to be a junior to get in her course, but she makes exceptions. I'll mention your name next time I see her." He smiled. His eyes were blue, not brown, but they twinkled like Daddy's.

I dreamed about Daddy. I dreamed that he came back, bursting through the door of the town house, his arms filled with pink packages. He'd finished his studying, he explained happily. He'd brought little pictures for the stark white walls: a woman poised in a seashell, her red hair trailing over pale breasts; an old man plucking a thorn from a lion's paw; a king surrounded by his court, the picture all dark red and satins. . . . I woke dumbly, the images fresh in my mind, and realized Daddy wasn't here, and the pictures were ones he'd shown me at breakfast back in Warrensburg. What if I'd looked more closely? What if I'd stayed up to watch the art specials on public TV, so he'd had someone to share his interest?

I waited for a letter. I'd dawdle on the way home from school, deliberately granting the mailman more time to reach into the bottom of his bag and find the letter with the forwarding address scrawled on the front. I wouldn't look through the stack of mail until I got inside the house and made myself a snack. Then I'd go through the envelopes one by one, and then, when it wasn't there, again.

"What are you looking for?" Cody asked, watching my ritual one afternoon.

"None of your business."

"I'd like to know how the Cubs are doing," Cody said. That was the name of his baseball team in Warrensburg.

"Uncle Mike could find out."

"I guess." His head was down, so I couldn't see his eyes.

"How come you didn't sign up here?"

He shrugged. "I don't get along with the kids."

"If you had something in common, maybe you would."

"I doubt it." Cody paused, as if he wondered whether he should tell me this: "I've decided I don't like people."

"Thanks a lot."

He grinned suddenly. Cody's smile can light up a room. "You and Mama are okay, and Uncle Mike."

"What about your friends back home?"

"They were talking about us, just like everybody else. I heard them."

"They don't talk about us here. Nobody knows us."

"But they're creeps, and they're dumb, too. They don't even know their water tastes bad, and the air stinks."

"I hope you didn't tell them."

"As a matter of fact, I did."

"Cody . . ." I shook my head, but it was more because I thought I should than that I really disapproved.

The one thing about Laglade that was *good* was Mama's job. Somehow she'd ended up in an office full of nice people. A couple of them had gone through separations or divorces, and they seemed to care about us even though they hardly knew us. Barb, whose kids were in high school, sent me a bag of clothes that blended in with what the other kids had. She sent Cody her son's old skateboard and helmet. And she told Mama about some land her uncle owned along a river in southern Pennsylvania. She and her kids used to camp there when they needed peace and quiet. "Barb asked her uncle, and he says it's fine for us to go there too," Mama said. "It's only an hour away. We can drive up this Saturday."

"We'll go fishing," I told Cody.

"What about worms?"

"Try the backyard."

He shook his head. "I scratched around out there when I was thinking of planting some tomatoes. It's artificial dirt."

"There's no such thing as artificial dirt."

"Sure there is. They sell it at the mall."

"Liar."

"It's in the aisle behind the plastic Christmas trees." He started laughing at his own dumb joke. But he got out the fishing rods, so we knew he wanted to go.

The river was called the Leanna, but the map was vague after we left the superhighway. We turned on a dirt road and jounced over deep ruts. After a mile the road dead-ended, and a trail led off to the left, through the woods. I saw new leaves on the oaks and poplars, but most of the trees were evergreens with long, sloping branches. They shaded the trail and made the under-cover dark and mossy. The path turned and headed steeply down. We picked our way over outcroppings of jagged rock. I could hear the river in the gorge below. Then, through the branches, I saw water. I dropped my pack and slid the rest of the way down to the river. Cody tumbled after me. The trees thinned and we ended up on a big flat rock with sunlight all around us.

The Leanna was small—not even seventy feet

across—and so clear you could see the bottom in most places. It was scattered with boulders that divided the water into channels and pools. The current was swift, and the deeper spots were tinged black. In the shallows, the water bubbled up gold and pink over the sand and stones.

Though it was pretty, I was disappointed. "It's more like a creek than a river."

"It's not like the Castle, that's for sure." Cody stood arms akimbo, his gaze measuring depth and flow. He shook his head. "Most of our lures won't work here, Sha."

"How come?"

"The current's fast, and there's not much surface in the main channels. They'll be swept downstream before they start jigging."

"Maybe it's wider somewhere else."

Cody nodded. His face looked relaxed, like he was back in his element, and what it relaxed from, I realized suddenly, was anger. I studied his expression. Did Cody miss Daddy? Did he want him to come back?

"Come get these packs," Mama called. "I can't carry everything."

We scrambled up to help her. She was surprised too at how small the Leanna was. "But it's nice, with the firs around it. I didn't realize how much I'd missed seeing green."

We found a flat rock for our gear and baited up. I

28

used a worm (Cody'd been right—we'd had to buy them), but Cody tied on a Mepps spinner, a tiny silver spoon with two hooks on the underside. He headed upstream. I went down.

It was different, all right. The banks held a jumble of boulders; just beyond them, a narrow path followed the curve of the stream. Little gray birds with black caps were singing at me in the evergreen branches. At home they would have been red-winged blackbirds.

I found a likely spot and tossed my line into a pool. The little red float wavered for a minute, then drifted downstream. Suddenly it disappeared. I jerked but there was nothing at the other end. "Snagged already?" I have a habit of talking to myself when I'm fishing. I yanked, walked downstream, pulled again, and the hook came free. I adjusted the float and cast again. This time the hook stayed off the bottom. I watched it float down, the worm wriggling over the rocky riverbed. I waited.

The moment the fish strikes is my favorite time. It's always a surprise; your heart starts thumping, and your hand flies to the crank on the reel. Is it a big one? The biggest yet? You have to keep the line tight while you wait for the fish to surface. Some bass will jump, but others, even big ones, are sluggish, and easy to get into the net. I hummed a little tune under my breath, cast again, changed bait. After a while the smell of woodsmoke drifted down the river, and my stomach growled. I packed my gear and went to find Mama.

She'd started the fire on a flat rock; there were hot dogs sizzling on some green sticks she'd cut, and a pan of beans nestled to one side. I was about to call Cody when he appeared upstream. He was grinning.

"I've got a surprise."

"What?"

"I'm not telling."

"Come on, Cody—"

He shrugged like it was nothing, but I could see he was excited. "I'll show you after lunch."

It didn't take us long to polish off the food. Mama scattered the fire and poured water on the loose coals. We headed upstream.

I didn't know what to expect, and Cody wasn't giving any hints, either. Beside us the river tumbled between rocks and ledges. We came around a curve where the left bank rose high and wide. In the mud by the river I saw coon tracks, and the sharp cloven prints of deer. Cody led us up and across a path that smelled of pine needles. He pointed triumphantly: "There!"

The cabin was hidden among trees, set against a dark, rocky wall. It was shaped like the little houses kids build with log construction sets, except that the logs were darker, almost black, and there was a big stone chimney on one end. The door was sagging on its hinges, but Cody pushed it open and ushered us in as if he owned the place. "Ta-daaah!"

You could tell it had once been nice. The main room

had a couple of windows that looked out on the river, but the glass was missing and the wood around them smelled like rot. There were some shelves built up against the near wall, and an old table with benches that were green with mold. The fireplace took up most of the far wall. A broad mantel held the bottom of a kerosene lamp.

"There's more!" Cody exclaimed. He led us through a doorway into a small dark room where beds with chicken-wire springs were built into the wall. Beside them a single window looked out onto the rocky cliff.

Cody showed us another opening off the main room. It must have been the pantry, because it was lined with shelves and drawers. There was even a window looking out toward the trees, and an old woodbox with rotting logs still inside it. A second door led outside, but it was stuck shut. "You have to come through the front and walk around," Cody explained.

We followed him dutifully. There was a spring out back, with a chipped enamel pail to catch the water. And hanging from a nail in the tree next to the spring was a metal cup. Granddaddy had hung a cup near our spring back home. "It's a way of telling travelers the water's good," he'd explained, and now and then we'd see someone stop, take down the cup, and drink. I reached for it now, but Mama stopped me. "We're trespassing, Shana. We don't know anything about this place."

"Except that it's abandoned," Cody said. "Look how the spring is clogged."

He was right about that: It was filled with rotting leaves. He rolled up his sleeves and cleared it out. Then he cupped some water in his hands and tossed it in the air. The drops caught a ray of sun and gleamed like diamonds. Magic, I thought. I looked around for more, but there was only the back of the cabin and, beyond it, the outhouse.

We were about to leave when two things happened. The first was that Cody told us something so unbelievable that I actually thought, even then, that it might come true. "This is where we're going to live this summer," he said.

Mama stared at him like he was crazy. She started saying all the things you knew a grown-up would say: We didn't know who owned the cabin and it wouldn't be safe, and the roof leaked, and everything we owned was in the town house, and there wasn't even a road to get here. I was waiting for her to finish, so I could put in my own two cents, when the cat appeared.

Four

My granddaddy believed in spirits. He believed they lived under water with the fish, and in the air, and also in the deep pools of your mind. "They rise at night, while you're sleeping, and tell you their secrets," he said. "If you listen, you can hear them."

"Do they look white, like ghosts?" I remember asking.

"You never know what shape they'll take." He sat looking off toward the river, his arms crossed over his round belly. "But they're there. When you're least expecting it, they'll come to you."

I asked Mama about that. She whispered that Granddad was old, and sometimes old people want to believe that life goes on forever. "So they imagine things that make it seem that way," she said. "You shouldn't argue with him."

I told Granddaddy what she said. He shook his head and laughed. "I know I'm going to die, Shana," he said. "I didn't say I believed in ghosts."

"You aren't going to die, either." I said. I held his hand tight.

Later I mostly forgot about spirits. I was too busy playing and reading and fishing, and also missing him. The cemetery was too far to visit without a car, so I made a little shrine down by the river, just a board with his name printed on it in Magic Marker and some pretty stones arranged around it in a circle. I didn't tell anybody, but I used to go there and talk to him. I'd ask how he was doing, and what heaven was like. He never answered, and over time I went there less and less. Before we moved to Laglade, I went looking for the spot. I had to hack away at weeds and vines before I found it. The board was mostly rotted, but the circle of stones was still there. I sat down and told Granddaddy what Daddy had done. I told him we were leaving his house and that it felt like the good we'd once had was crumbling the way the old tobacco shed behind the house had rotted, tilted, and finally just fallen apart. I could hear the murmur of the river to my right. I waited to see if Granddaddy would speak to me, but if he did, I couldn't hear what he said. I felt like a book filled with blank pages, waiting for my story to be written by someone else.

On the other hand, Cody was certain about everything. He was sure that Daddy had betrayed us; if he came back, Cody didn't want to see him. Cody knew for a fact that Laglade was the worst place on earth, that nobody should have to live there, and that those who chose to were idiots. He was just as sure that the cabin was where we were meant to be: no people, no roads, just us and the river.

And the cat, who had emerged from a clump of rocks just as we were about to leave. He was an old orange tom, with a head the size of a softball and patchy fur covered with burrs. He was thin but proud; he didn't wheedle. Instead he leaped lightly into the empty window frame and stood peering out, as if to ask: Did I invite you in? He let me rub his head before he moved away and sat staring with yellow eyes.

"We can't just leave him here," I said.

"We can't take him, either. The lease says no pets." Mama was firm, but she looked concerned. "Where do you suppose he came from?"

"Who knows?" Cody was kneeling, holding out one hand. "But he's on his own, that's for sure."

"We can't leave him here," I said again. "He'll starve."

"He's not starving now. He probably catches mice in the cabin."

I didn't expect it, but I started to cry. I couldn't just walk away from him.

"We'll leave some food," Mama said briskly. "Cody, run back to the rock and look in my pack. There're some extra hot dogs there, and some cheese slices. When we get home, I'll ask Barb if she knows who owns the cabin, and if the cat is theirs."

Who owned the cabin was George Cosgrove, Barb's uncle, but he didn't know a thing about the cat. The cabin, he said, we could use in trade for the repairs it needed. He and his wife had moved to a retirement home, but they'd hated the thought of selling the place along the river 'cause they'd had good times there when they were young. Mama couldn't believe it when Barb told her. "Don't you and your children want to use it?" she asked.

"No, my kids don't want to leave their social life," Barb said. "Now that they're in high school, they have dates or parties almost every Saturday."

Not like us, I thought when Mama told me. I was still trying to figure out whether I wanted anything to do with that beat-up cabin. But Warrensburg was six hours away, and Uncle Mike didn't have a guest room in his tiny apartment. What would I do in Laglade once school let out? Wait for the mail to come? Watch TV? Go to the pool? The thought of the other girls looking at me pale and skinny in my bathing suit made me cringe. Maybe I'd be better off in the woods with Cody.

Then there was the cat—our cat, I called him in my mind. I'd worried about him ever since we'd left. Had he eaten the food we'd piled by the rocks where we'd first seen him? Was he waiting for us to come back?

Mama made Cody work for what he wanted. Before she'd consider the cabin, he'd have to show he'd done his homework every night for the last two weeks of school, and there couldn't be any pink slips from the teacher, either. Not only that, but he had to invite a friend for supper. Cody went down the row of desks in his class inviting kids until one girl said yes. She spent the whole evening talking about the day she met the star of *General Hospital* at the opening of Hillcrest Mall. Cody lied a lot. "Hillcrest's my favorite mall too," he told her. Mama nearly killed him after she left.

That weekend we sat down and talked about the problems with Cody's idea. We'd found a closer road in, but Mama'd still have to commute an hour, then walk the last half mile to the cabin. There was a house near where she'd park on the other side of the trail; the owner, Mrs. Burns, said we could use the phone for emergencies. But Mama still felt uneasy. "What if one of you gets hurt?" she asked. "You'd be left alone while the other one hiked to the phone. You could lie there for an hour."

"That's no different from back home," Cody argued. "We were gone all day when we went fishing. Sometimes we were miles from any house."

"That's true." Mama nodded. "But this is a strange place. There could be dangers we don't know about."

"Like what? Tigers? Quicksand?" Cody grinned.

Mama turned to me. "What do you think, Shana?"

I was pleased she'd asked my opinion, and I tried to sound grown-up and logical. "It'd be pretty boring being here all summer. You'd be gone all day, and there's not much to do without a car. I guess we'd just stay inside and watch TV."

"Some of those shows are so violent." Mama sighed. "Maybe you would be better off outdoors."

"We'd be careful," Cody said. "*Real* careful. I wouldn't do anything without asking Shana."

Mama didn't answer, but she looked right at me. "That's a lot of responsibility."

"I think I can handle it. I'll have some schoolwork— Mr. Thomas told me to keep a journal, and he gave out a summer reading list, too. I could work in the morning, and after lunch Cody and I'd go fishing."

"I'd want you to know exactly where Cody was," Mama said. "And the two of you'd have to be back in time to make supper. I couldn't get there before six, with the drive."

Cody could tell he'd almost won. "We'll make the

best food you ever tasted—fried chicken and ham and even broccoli, if that's what you want."

Mama smiled, but she kept looking at me. Cody kicked me under the table. I gave him a look that said, *You owe me.* "We'll be careful, Mama. It'll work out fine."

"I'm trusting you, Shana."

I nodded, like there was nothing to it.

Later that night she told us we could go. She'd written out some rules: no swimming alone; tell each other where you're going and when you'll be back; be at the cabin by five to fix supper. We'd have to boil the water from the spring until the state sent back test results from a sample Mama planned to give them. A week later I stood gazing at the loaded car, parked as close to the cabin as we could get it.

"Do we really need this much plastic?" Cody hoisted a thick roll over one shoulder. "Did you remember the staple gun? What about my box of Milky Ways?"

Mama was juggling a broom and a bag of potatoes. "For heaven's sake, Cody, be still." She frowned at me. "Shana, you have to carry something besides your library books."

"I am!" I grabbed a plastic grocery bag and picked up a bedroll, too. The pile sticking out of the trunk seemed bigger than ever. "This is going to take lots of trips."

"What did you expect? You're the one who kept adding stuff."

"Shut up, Cody." I started off. This trail approached the cabin from a different direction, angling across the gorge more gradually. When I saw the glint of water, I knew from the map to turn right. The path was choked with weeds. I beat them down with the grocery bag, wondering why I'd agreed to this. I shifted my books to the other arm and saw the roof of the cabin below me. I climbed down and stood in front of it. The doorway gaped, and I noticed a vine growing from the sagging gutter. I piled my load neatly in the yard and called the cat. I called again, but he didn't come.

Mama and I cleaned while Cody fetched our things. We started out sweeping, and once we'd cleared the leaves and sticks, we brushed the walls and ceilings, knocking down cobwebs, spiders, even a bird's nest. I scrubbed the shelves and table with vinegar and water, and Mama cut squares of clear plastic for the empty windows. We stapled the tops but taped the lower sections so they could be rolled up on hot days. Then Mama showed me how to cut screening, and we stapled that to the outside window frames. I built a little fire in the fireplace to dry out the damp, but Mama said until the roof was patched that smell was going to be there, and she hadn't had space to bring a pail of pitch.

What we had brought was piled outside now, and

Cody and I started to put it away: quilts and pillows in the back room; kerosene lanterns, one for the mantel, the other for the bedroom. Our propane camp stove went on the widest shelf, next to a water basin and a bucket. We hammered nails to hang our cast-iron frying pan and two cook pots, little and big; mess kits, matches, and a portable radio sat beside the stove. We'd brought two fruit crates for Cody's and my clothes, and a flashlight for each of us.

We sprayed the pantry for bugs, then washed it down before we put the food away. Mama had brought bread and peanut butter and honey, cereal and powdered milk, oranges and rice, baked beans and pretzel sticks. There were cans of soup, crackers, cookies, Vienna sausages, and beef stew. Mama would buy fresh meat or cheese on her way from work, since we had no way to keep them cold. A half-dozen eggs and a little tub of butter could rest in the stone alcove beside the spring.

I hung my nightshirt from a nail beside my bed and arranged my library books on top of the wooden box, which I'd painted blue the night before. On his crate Cody had piled his pocketknife, a compass, a bunch of comic books, and some string. Mama would sleep on a cot in the main room. She'd strung a rope with a curtain over it across one corner, for privacy.

"Shana—baby mice!" Cody found them nestled in a wad of sawdust under the eaves. Their pink bodies squirmed helplessly. He carried them outdoors and set them in a crevice between stones. "Have you seen the cat?" he asked anxiously.

"I called, but he didn't come."

"Hope he doesn't find these guys."

"I hope they stay out of our food!"

"There're metal boxes for the stuff that isn't canned."

"This is going to be like camping, isn't it?"

"It's going to be *good*," Cody said.

It was almost time to make supper. We walked through the house, inspecting our work. Mama'd spread a pretty cloth over the table; that and the curtain around her cot gave a touch of color to the front room. The lantern on the mantel, the pots on the wall felt cozy, even though there was no place to sit except the benches. The pantry, with its row of canned goods and metal grub boxes, was orderly, and though the bedroom was small, it was neater than Cody's or my room had ever been. We made a list of things we'd forgotten: another water bucket, caulk to patch the holes in the chinking between logs, extra batteries for the flashlights. Tonight, since it was Saturday, Mama said she'd make supper. "Why don't you go for a little walk, to shake the dust off?" she suggested.

We went down to the river. The light was different, because it was evening. The water gleamed; flecks of foam scudded like little boats down miniature rapids.

Cody lay on his stomach and threw sticks into the current, watching them twist and dodge. After a while he sat up and looked at me. "This is the first good thing that's happened since Daddy left," he said.

"Speak for yourself," I said, though I was happy too, partly because of the cabin but also for a reason no one else knew.

"I want to live here forever."

I laughed, feeling pleasure at his happiness. But I couldn't let him be.

"You can't spend your life hiding from people," I said.

"I can spend my life however I want to."

"Once you're grown, maybe . . . but you'll have to have a job, won't you?"

"Nope. I can fish and hunt, and have a garden for my vegetables. I'll have an apple tree, too, so I can make pies." Cody smacked his lips.

"I think I'll be a writer," I said. "That way I can live wherever I like. I could even live in Europe if I wanted to."

"Europe!" Cody's mouth turned as sour as a sour apple. I knew he was thinking of Daddy.

"For all you know it might be nice over there," I said. "Maybe it's nicer than here."

"No. Europe is full of people."

"And museums and castles and cathedrals."

"A river is better," Cody said.

We sat for a while, resting. I was waiting to hear Mama call, and finally she did.

We climbed the wall of the gorge, being careful because there was no path. Mama had heated stew and made bannock bread in the frying pan. The table was set with the metal plates and flatware from our mess kits. Though it was still light out, the front room was shadowed, so Cody lit the kerosene lamp and set it on the table. Mama said grace, and I let my lips move along with her words.

"The cat hasn't come back," Cody said suddenly.

"He's probably a wanderer," Mama said. "He may have a circuit he travels. And I'll bet this is one of his stops."

We boiled water and cleaned up the dishes. Then I sat at the table and read by lamplight, while Cody listened to the radio. I poured water from the bucket to wash my face and hands. Afterward, when I went outside to dump the dirty water, I saw that the swath of sky over the river was alive with glimmering stars.

I went to bed feeling lucky. Cody has chosen what was best for us. And in the pocket of my jeans, grabbed from the mailbox in Laglade before anyone else could see it, was a letter from Daddy.

Five

I read the letter when I was alone by the river. Before I opened it, I examined the envelope carefully, writing down the return address: 229 W. 79th St., Apt. 21B, New York, N.Y. The letter had been sent to Warrensburg; the postmistress, Mrs. Grubb, had printed our new address on the right side of the envelope just below my name: Shana Allen. Daddy had written to me, I knew, because I was the one who'd been waiting so patiently for his letter and who knew he would come back. *Shana darling*, the letter began:

What a wonderful day I've spent! I began at the Metropolitan Museum, only a fifteen-minute walk from my basement apartment. There I sat in front of a Raphael masterpiece, soaking in the rich colors and complex themes of that superb painting. Later I walked to the Frick Museum, which also contains several Renaissance paintings. Viewing the real art instead of the prints I saw in library books is wonderful. You can almost imagine the artist standing there in front of you, paintbrush in hand!

Shana, how are you and Cody and Dot getting along? I think of you all the time, and wish you could be here with me. My apartment is just one room, which I get rent free in exchange for being a security guard at night.

I'll write again soon.

Love and kisses,
Daddy

I read the letter a dozen times. I wished it was longer! There were a million questions I wanted to ask: What's your apartment like? How did you get a job? Where do you buy groceries? When will you come home? I fingered the single page. Why hadn't Daddy put his phone number? Then I could have found some change and gone to a pay phone. But maybe he didn't have money for a telephone. . . . I'll write to him, I decided.

My letter took up most of Monday. For some reason, I didn't want Cody to know about it, or about Daddy's letter: not yet. That meant I had to hide them every time he got near. I also had to think up an excuse for

46

not doing whatever he wanted me to: going fishing, going for a hike, looking for the cat. Finally I told him I had a headache and wanted to be by myself. He looked at me like he didn't believe me, but he went off to explore the river farther up.

I rewrote my letter to Daddy four times. It ended up like this:

Dear Daddy,

It was great to get your letter!

Mama and Cody and I moved! We are mostly living in a town house in Laglade, Md. Our address is 219 Hamlin Way, Laglade, 21236. Our new phone number is 301-555-6742.

Even though we moved, we're not staying in the town house over the summer, because Cody hated it. So we're staying at a cabin in Pennsylvania, on the Leanna River. We don't have electricity, running water, or telephone, so it's like camping. You would love it—the river is pretty, with evergreens all around.

Please tell me: How did you get to New York? What's it like? Do you have another job besides security guard? Do you have a phone?

Daddy, I'm glad you're getting to see the artwork from the Renaissance. But Cody and I miss you very much.

Your loving daughter,
Shana

I read my letter over and folded it up. I had an envelope with a stamp on it stuck in one of my library books; I'd mail it over the weekend, when we went out to shop. I carried the letter up to the cabin and hid it in the book. Cody had boiled water and made Kool-Aid, and I drank a glass, feeling uneasy. Why didn't I want Mama or Cody to see Daddy's letter, or mine? Was I lying to keep it a secret? Why hadn't I asked Daddy the most important question of all?

"Shana, come quick!" Cody's voice was almost a scream. I ran out the door. He was standing partway up the path, his hands raised high. Below him, on a rock beside the river, stood an old man in a khaki uniform. It took me a second to see the gun in his right hand.

"Stop!" I shouted.

The man looked up, startled, and dropped the gun. It hit the rock and bounced somewhere along the bank. He cursed and bent over, looking for it. Cody scrambled up the slope and grabbed me, pulling me toward the cabin.

"He's crazy, Shana! Run!"

I turned, but as I did I glanced down and saw that the old man was on all fours, groping on the ground. His head bobbed as if he hardly had the strength to hold it up, and there was a naked pink spot in the middle of his thin white hair.

"Shana, come *on*!" Cody was yanking at my arm.

"Just a second."

The old man looked up and saw me watching. "You better get down here and help me, girl!" he bellowed. "That gun is worth eighty-three dollars, and if it's lost, it's your fault!"

"It's not my fault either! You were aiming it at my brother!"

"That's 'cause he's not supposed to be here, and neither are you. I'm giving you exactly one hour to get off this property before I arrest you for trespassing!"

"We aren't trespassing. We have the owner's permission to be here."

"What owner?"

"Mr. George Cosgrove."

The old man staggered to his feet. His empty hands clenched, like he was getting ready for a fight. "George Cosgrove has no right to give anybody permission to mess up this river, or to camp anywhere near it, or to stay in that old cabin of his. He should have told you that from the start."

"Why?"

"What do you mean, why? Don't you know anything?"

"I told you, he's *crazy*," Cody muttered from behind me.

"Why?" I repeated.

" 'Cause this is a trout stream, and the land around it is federally protected land. You can't walk here, you can't camp here, you can't do anything here."

"You mean nobody can come here?"

"That's right." The old man nodded as if finally I'd shown a grain of sense. "Nobody."

"What about you?"

He bristled again, and his chest swelled as if he'd swallowed something big. "I'm the ranger. I enforce the law."

"I bet you aren't supposed to be pointing your gun at people."

He turned red. "That boy is a bad boy. I told him to stop, and he kept on running."

"He isn't bad either. He just didn't know."

"Now he does." He crossed his arms. I could see printing over the left pocket of his shirt, but I was too far away to make out what it said. "Come help me find my gun!" he yelled.

"I will not! You could have hurt Cody, or me."

"I couldn't either. It isn't even loaded."

"Then you shouldn't aim it like it is!"

"You better help me. If you don't, I'm going to have you arrested."

"What for?"

He paused, as if I'd caught him. He licked his lips. "For insubordination. Not only that, but I'll tell your parents you were here."

"Not Mama," Cody whispered. "She won't let us stay if she finds out."

"How will you tell them?"

"How the heck do you think? I'll come up there."
He pointed toward the cabin.

"They're not here now."

"Later."

"But if I find the gun, you won't?"

He hesitated, thinking it over. "No."

"All right. But you better not point it at Cody or me
or anyone else."

He muttered something I couldn't hear.

"You stay here," I told Cody. I scrambled down the
rocky slope till I was only a few feet away from him.
Up close I saw he was even older than I'd thought; his
eyes were glassy, and the skin hung around his neck in
loose jowls, like an old bulldog. His shirt was worn and
so faded that it was hard to read the writing:

PA. F SH H   CH

"Over here," he growled.

I searched in the low underbrush near the rock while
he stood watching. It didn't take me thirty seconds to
see the black barrel of the pistol. I picked it up by the
handle and held it out at arm's length.

"You found it," he grunted. He stuck it in his pants
pocket and glared at me. "I'm not telling your parents,
but I am going to issue a citation," he said.

"What's that?"

"It's a notice of violation of the law. I send it to the
federal government."

"We haven't done anything wrong!"

"You should have known you can't stay in that cabin. Privies are illegal near the river. They pollute the water."

I stood there with my mouth open. "What are we supposed to do?"

"Get out," he said. He turned and limped away.

I practically dragged Cody into the cabin. I shoved him down on the bench and started yelling. "You better tell me everything that happened! What did you do to make him mad?"

"Shana . . ." Cody's face was white, and he looked like he was close to tears. "It's not my fault."

"Tell me everything, before Mama gets home!"

He sighed and started in.

"Since you wouldn't do anything, I figured I'd go upstream and find a good fishing spot. I hiked up about a mile and saw a couple nice, deep places. I cleared away the brush around them so they'd be easy to get to. Farther up, I came across a cliff with a little cave in it. I found some bones and hunks of fur, so I thought a wildcat might be living there. Then I thought I heard it! I scrambled up to the top of the cliff and ran along the edge. I could hear something crying upstream. Then I remembered the cat!"

Cody shook his head miserably. "I crossed the river to the other side. Around the bend I saw a canoe pulled up in the underbrush. I thought maybe it had swept downriver in high water—remember how that used to happen back home when there was a flood?"

I nodded.

"Well, I turned it over—I hadn't forgotten about the cat, I just thought I'd investigate the canoe first. Then somebody shouted. I stood up and waited, so I could explain, when that old guy came stomping through the trees screaming, 'Thief! Thief!' He wouldn't shut up. Finally I just took off running. I figured I'd outdistance him in a couple minutes, 'cause he's so old."

"You shouldn't have started running," I said. "That made him think you were guilty."

"Guilty of what? Touching his boat?" Cody shrugged, and went on: "Anyway, I hurried on back, thinking I'd tell you about the cat. I was just a hundred yards up-stream from here when he came around the bend in the boat. As soon as he saw me, he beached it and pulled out the gun. That's when I started yelling."

I stared at Cody to see if he was lying, but he didn't blink or turn red. Instead he groaned and buried his face in his hands. "I heard what he said to you, Shana. What are we going to do?"

"I don't know. You start supper while I think."

I tried to sort it out. The old man had a gun, and probably bullets, wherever he lived. It made sense that a ranger would have a gun: You never knew when you'd come across a sick animal that had to be put out of its misery. Still, rangers weren't supposed to use their guns against people, especially kids. Had Cody really done anything that bad?

"What are you making?" I asked him, trying to slow the whirlwind of arguments in my head.

"Sausage and potatoes. There's a jar of applesauce we can have, too. Mama'll like that, won't she, Shana?"

"Mama," I muttered, nodding to Cody. On the hillside he'd whispered that she wouldn't let us stay. That was true—no parents would let their kids live near a lunatic. We'd move back to the town house. I'd hate that, and Cody would too. But if we stayed and he got shot, it would be my fault. . . .

"Shana, Mama'll be here soon." I knew what Cody was trying to ask, but I couldn't answer, not yet.

"Did you set the table?"

He nodded, his thin face twitching with nervousness. It would hurt him to go back, but it might kill him to stay.

"Did you decide?" he asked.

"Not yet."

"I won't go up there again if you don't tell. I swear."

"He knows we're here, Cody."

"He's old. Maybe he'll forget."

We heard footsteps outside, the door was drawn aside, and Mama came in.

Six

Dinner was quiet. We asked Mama about her day before she could ask about ours, and made small talk to fill in the spaces. Still, when she pushed back her plate and asked, "What happened today?" I wasn't sure what to say.

But Cody was. He told her about his walk, spreading it out as if it might have taken all day, and leaving out the cat noises and the ranger. When he finished, I couldn't help staring at him. I'd never known he was that good a liar.

"What about you, Shana?"

I took a deep breath, for my story'd have to cover up not only the ranger but Daddy's letter, and mine to him. "I spent most of the day reading," I muttered. "The book was just so good I couldn't put it down."

"What book was that?" Cody asked sharply, and I saw he'd realized I was hiding something from him, too.

I glared. "It's a suspense novel. The title is *Katie Spills the Beans*."

"I think I've heard of it," Cody said.

"I'll wash the dishes," I mumbled, and I got up and moved away.

We spent the next day hanging around the cabin. I helped Cody scramble up on the roof, where he poked around trying to find the leaks. The metal flashing near the chimney was rusty, he called. "Want me to bust it out?"

"Not till we have something to fix it with, dummy."

"The tarpaper's worn through up here too, Shana. You can see into the bedroom if you put your eye up close."

"Mama said she'd try to get some pitch at the hardware store."

"Remember that time Mama and Daddy patched the roof at home, and I got tar on my shoe and couldn't get it off?"

"That's 'cause you stuck your foot in the bucket."

"Yeah." Cody grinned from up above me. "I don't know how old I was, but I do remember thinking,

Should I? And before I could think it through, I did."

"You didn't want to think it through."

"When you think too much, you miss all the fun."

"Yeah, Cody—like yesterday."

His face got tight. "What would you have done?"

"I would have stood my ground and explained that I wasn't doing anything to his boat."

"He probably would have shot you on the spot. Only reason he didn't shoot me was 'cause there was a witness."

"I don't know about that. He said the gun wasn't loaded."

Cody slid to the edge of the roof, spun around, and hung from the overhang by his hands. He dropped. "Maybe it was, maybe it wasn't, but I'm not going back up there, I can tell you that."

"Good." For once, I thought, Cody has learned his lesson.

We built a fire outside and made hamburgers for lunch. There was a smooth patch of ground about fifteen feet from the cabin door where we built our campfire ring. While we were gathering stones, Cody found two salamanders: one with a blue streak and another with a gold body and black spots. We put some wet leaves in the washbasin, and they burrowed underneath them and wouldn't come out. We named them Shy and Spot. Cody was so busy playing with them that he didn't help me clean up the dishes, and when I said he'd have to do it after supper, he acted like he didn't hear.

Later, as if it had been listening when Cody was on the roof, thunder rumbled. We unrolled the windows and taped them down, hoping the dark clouds overhead would scud on by. Suddenly a wind blew down the side of the gorge, tossing dirt and stones in front of it. In the half-light the pines and hemlocks looked menacing, and lightning clattered in the strip of sky above the river. The cabin, on its shelf of dirt and rock, felt tiny and exposed. I lit the lamp and took a book from the crate beside my bed. Cody turned on the radio, but there was only static.

"The rain's coming," he said, standing by the front window. "Shana, look!"

Along the river a line of rain advanced like the steady silent march of an army. As it drew abreast of us, the storm hit the house. The plastic on the windows bulged, then tore loose; and rain hurtled through. "Quick, more tape!" Cody yelled.

"Where is it?"

"I put it right there!" He pointed to the mantel.

"If you had, it would be there!"

"Hurry, Shana . . ." Cody was trying to hold the plastic shut. I found the tape on the table, but by then the sill was too wet for it to stick. All we could do was stand there and watch the rain pour in.

"Oh my God—the roof!" The water must have pooled up there before the floodgates opened, and it began to stream down the wall beside the fireplace. In the bedroom, two spots were spouting like open faucets. We set a bucket and a pot under them. "At least it didn't get the quilts," I said.

"Not *yet*." Cody surveyed the ceiling there for drips.

"This pot's full."

"Dump it in the washbasin."

"I can't—we put the salamanders in there."

He made a face. "The front room's flooded—you can empty it there."

"Maybe I'll dump it on *you*."

He grinned. "I wouldn't mind a shower, now that you mention it."

"Cody!"

But he was stripping off his clothes. A second later he ran into the big room in his underwear, a bar of soap in one hand. I lugged the water in after him, watching as he lathered up by the open window. "La . . . di . . . da . . ." Cody was hamming it up. He stuck his hands over his head and twirled around like a ballerina. "Hit me, Shana!" he shouted. I aimed the pot of water at his bony chest. *Splat!* He roared. I ran into the bedroom and got the bucket.

"Get my butt!" Cody yelled, spinning around.

I aimed and let fly. *Splat!* Cody screeched. He kicked up his heels and crowed like a rooster. The rain beat in through the windows, and thunder rumbled somewhere up the river.

The rain kept on for a half hour. By the time it slowed, Cody and I were trying to clean up. The cabin floor looked like a lake, and both of us were drenched.

Then Cody started shivering so bad his teeth chattered. I told him to get in bed while I made a fire. The wood was wet and wouldn't light, but then I remembered the dry stuff in the woodbox in the pantry. I managed to tear off some bark and twigs and get them started. The dry wood flamed right up, but when I added wet it hissed and steamed. By the time the fire was blazing, I was in no mood to tackle the wet floor. And we'd promised Mama we'd make supper, too.

"Cody, come help!" I called.

"I'm too cold."

"Then come in here and warm up."

He did, wrapping the quilt around him like a bathrobe. I moved a bench in front of the fireplace, and he stretched his bare legs toward the flames. I got the broom and tried sweeping the pools of water out the door. That cleared most of it up. The rest I soaked up with our towels while Cody watched.

"What if I need to dry off?" he asked.

"You should have thought of that before you took your clothes off."

"I can't think of everything," he whined.

I felt my face get red. When Cody was little, I used

to hit him and he'd hit me back, but we hadn't done that for a couple of years. Instead I slammed the broom down on the floor. "You better start helping!" I yelled. "What do you think I am, your damn servant?"

He grinned suddenly. "Servants don't cuss."

"Cody! Stop joking and help me!"

"What if I don't?"

It came out before I thought about it. "I'll tell Mama about yesterday."

He sat straight up. "You better not! Anyway, you lied too."

"To cover for you."

"No way. You said you'd spent the whole day reading."

I stiffened. "So what? I was down by the river writing. I told you I wanted to be a writer, remember?"

"Then why'd you lie?"

"I'm writing a poem for Mama, and I want it to be a surprise."

Cody stared sullenly. "You just thought that up this minute."

I crossed my arms and glared back. "Prove it."

We made the supper together, Cody doing what I told him but with a mean expression. Then when Mama got home he acted nice as pie. He showed her Spot and Shy and described the storm, pointing out the leaks and talking about how we'd get them patched. She had no idea how bad it had really been, and we didn't tell.

Because in the past few days, something had changed between the three of us. Cody and I had lied about the ranger so we could stay at the cabin. Whatever we faced, we faced on our own, and the outcome, good or bad, was up to us.

The next morning I did try to write a poem. I took a pencil and a book of poetry down to the river and sat leafing through the pages for inspiration. Back in my English class in Laglade, Catherine had said the poems she wrote came to her like songs. But my mind felt empty—dry and brittle as an autumn leaf.

"Shana?" Cody was standing on the little bluff above me. "Want to go fishing?"

"I'm writing," I lied.

"How about later?"

"Why don't you go by yourself?"

"I could. . . . It's just . . . I thought you might want to."

You're afraid of the ranger, I thought, but I didn't say it out loud. "I'll call you when I'm ready."

"Good! I'll get our tackle."

Once the idea of fishing was in my head, it wouldn't let go, and the blank paper in front of me began to seem like something that had drifted in on the wind. Still, I made myself wait a good ten minutes, holding on to the pencil to see if it would suddenly come to life. It didn't. I trudged up to the cabin and put my stuff away. Cody had made sandwiches: peanut butter on white bread. We wrapped them in a plastic bag with a couple of oranges and took off. I wanted to go down the river, but Cody said no: "The best spots are upstream."

"Are you crazy? That's where you saw the boat."

He shook his head. "The canoe was a half mile beyond the place I want to go. And there's plenty of spots to hide, if we hear him coming."

He was right about the fishing; the pools were deep and clear. We started out fifty feet apart, me working one bank and him the other. We'd cast into the eddies and let the lures drift down where the current could take them. I tried a Rapala minnow and then a rooster-tail. Then I changed to a size-five hook with a worm on it. That got me a hard swift tug. A minute later I pulled in a little sucker.

"Gross!" Cody yelled. He hates suckers. I flipped it off the hook and threw it back.

Cody thought we were doing something wrong. We sat on the bank eating sandwiches while he talked. "I think it's the bait," he said. "We're used to fish that live in slower water, like at home."

"Granddaddy would have known. . . . I bet he caught trout."

Cody shook his head. "I looked in the picture box, but I only saw bass and catfish."

"The picture box . . ." I'd forgotten about the bent-up cardboard box where we kept the family photographs. Last time I'd seen it was back in Warrensburg, on the shelf beside Daddy's notebooks. Birthdays, Christmases, trophy fish, sunsets, the first flowers of spring, Granddaddy even after he got sick—they were all in the picture box. "Where is it?" I asked Cody.

"Under my bed."

"You snuck it up here?"

"I didn't *sneak* it—I brought it."

"How come?"

He looked embarrassed. "Because I like to look at the pictures."

"Is the picture of Daddy in his chaps and boots in there? The one Mel took at the rodeo?"

Cody nodded.

"I always loved that picture." I sat staring at the crust of my sandwich. Something inside me hurt, and I tried to steady it. "You miss Daddy too, don't you Cody?"

"I guess—I don't know. Why do you ask such dumb questions?"

"Because I've been thinking."

"What?"

"Mama really likes her new job, and she's making more money than she was. I'm afraid she won't want to go home when Daddy comes back."

Cody stared at me like he never thought about this stuff. "She did say the town house was easier to keep clean," he said.

64

"And they're training her so she can get a promotion. If she does, she'll be a manager. I heard her tell Uncle Mike on the phone."

"Managers can transfer."

"But not to Warrensburg. Remember old Mr. Weiss? He's been the manager there for a million years."

"I'll have to think about that." Cody sighed, wriggled, turned back toward me. "Know what, Sha? I keep hearing that cat."

"Now?"

He shook his head sheepishly. "In my mind. The thing is, it sounded hurt."

"No way am I—"

"I have a plan." Cody kept on. "Once we're near the canoe, we'll stay on the other bank and circle around till we're way upstream. If we don't hear anything, we'll come right back here. That cat's probably gone by now, like he left us. I just have to be sure."

"You don't know it's our same cat, Cody. You don't even know it is a cat."

"Nothing bad is going to happen," Cody said. "I swear."

We hid our fishing gear behind a log and went upstream. Cody pointed out the cave he'd found earlier. Farther on we saw the metal gleam of the canoe. We crouched, listened: nothing. We cut back like Cody'd planned, making a half-circle through the woods.

The place we came out was different: The river was

wider and calm, bordered by a grove of birches. Way back the gorge rose green and gray. We heard only the gentle riffling of the water between broad, low banks. "We'll go back," Cody whispered, and we did. From deep in the woods I still thought I could see the glimmer of metal against the other shore.

We'd gotten back to the cave when the cat cried out. I wanted to pretend I hadn't heard. Then it came again, a strange, hurt noise from the far side of the river.

We crossed downstream and headed north, bending low and running one at a time through clusters of broad-leafed shrubs—rhododendron, Mama'd called it. We took cover under a rock overhang. "I'll be back," Cody said.

"Wait!"

But he was gone. The cat cried again, a long thin howl.

"Cody!" I whispered.

His head appeared in a window of light in front of the rock. "I know where it's coming from. There's a cliff a couple hundred feet behind the canoe. It's there."

"The ranger's going to catch us, Cody." My heart was pounding.

"I have to find it," Cody said.

"Then I'm going with you."

We planned our route—from the rock to a clump of evergreens to another group of rocks beside the cliff— and we scrambled one at a time, Cody first, staying as low to the ground as we could. Besides the canoe there were no signs of people, and I began to think we might be all right. The cat howled again, somewhere close and to our right.

We had to pass a clearing between the cliff and the river. We went together, still crouched, hoping the cat would cry out to guide us. We looked along the cliff wall and in the high weeds and grass. A line of cedars blocked the view to our right. We darted behind the thick low branches of the closest one. On the other side, almost completely hidden by the trees, was a small cabin.

"His," Cody muttered. His voice rattled like dry leaves.

"Maybe he's not there."

The cat cried again. We sank to our bellies and crawled through the high grass, the tree trunks like a fence between us and the house. We could see his backyard: a garden with flowers and a birdhouse. A couple of paddles leaned against a wooden shed. Beside them were some tools and a roll of chicken wire. A pump handle stuck up from a concrete cistern. An overturned bucket sat next to it on the bare earth.

The cat howled. We crawled along the tree line until we could see behind the shed, and there he was, our cat, his big orange head looking right at us.

He was in a metal cage, and on the door was a padlock.

Seven

When he saw us, the cat shrank against the far wall of the cage. Cody pulled on the lock, but it wouldn't budge.

I glanced toward the cabin. Had something moved there, in the window?

"He's got food and water," I said nervously. "The cage isn't against the law."

"This isn't his cat." Cody kept pulling on the lock.

"How do you know?"

His shoulders squared as if he was getting ready for a fight. "I just know."

I kept my eyes on the window. "Hurry up, Cody."

"I can't get it. We'll have to find the key."

"You want me to knock on the door and ask for it?

What do I say: This time we're here to steal your cat?"

Cody didn't answer me. He talked to the cat, to calm it down. He was rubbing its head through the bars.

"Come on." I gestured toward the line of evergreens. "We'll hide there and figure out what to do."

What we planned was this: I'd knock on his door, say we'd heard a cat and that ours was lost. If he got nasty, I'd put up my hands and walk away. If he wasn't home, I'd see if the cabin door was locked. Maybe the key to the padlock was hanging just inside. We could "borrow" it, free the cat, and carry him downriver. As long as we returned the key, there'd be no way to prove we'd done anything wrong.

"What if we can't find it?" Cody thought out loud. "Or what if he finds us?"

"Bang," I said. I flicked my index finger like it was a gun. Neither of us laughed. "Any other ideas?"

Cody shook his head.

"Then I'll go. You watch from here."

His cabin was smaller than ours but nicer, with big windows and a wide front porch. Peeking in, I saw that the main room contained a potbellied stove, a chair, a desk, and his bed. Against the back wall the kitchen table held a chipped pot filled with red geraniums. Books and papers were stacked beside it; next to them was a collection of dirty plates and mugs. There was no one home. I knocked, just to be sure. Then I tried the door. As if it were waiting for me, it swung open.

I didn't want to go in, and I don't know why I did, because usually I don't do crazy things. My whole life I've been the one who followed the rules. This is against the law, the voice in the back of my mind whispered. . . . There wasn't any key hanging on the wall near the door. I pushed through the clutter, toward the back. There was a bathroom and a pantry, like ours, stuck on the rear of the house, and the main room formed an L to accomodate an iron sink and dish cupboard. The log walls were hung with river maps and charts of fish, all of them grubby and covered with notes. A fishing rod and a couple pairs of waders slumped in one corner.

"Hurry," Cody called from outside.

"Is he coming?"

"No, not yet . . ."

Then I saw a key hanging from a nail in the back door frame. Please let it be the one, I prayed, and I took it out back, almost tripping over another pot of flowers set square on the steps there. The key fit. I opened the cage. Cody gathered the cat to him. "Run!" I said. "I'll meet you back at the cabin." He did run too, the cat's front legs draped around his neck like a baby's arms.

I returned the key and made sure the doors were closed. Before I left, I glanced through the front window. With its hodgepodge of dishes, charts, books, and flowers, the cabin drew me like a magnet; but this time common sense prevailed, and I hurried away, toward the river. The canoe was where we'd left it, pulled up and chained to an iron spike. I followed a path that led downstream. I was in such a hurry, I almost ran right into him.

The ranger didn't hear me coming. He was crouched over the riverbank, holding a plastic tube in both hands. I couldn't decide whether to back up or talk to him. Then he looked up and saw me.

"Seventy-one degrees, and the sedimentation is moderate," he said, as if we were friends. "I would have expected worse, after that rain Wednesday. I guess the low-pressure zone wasn't as big as the radio said." He wrote something down in a pocket notebook. Then he looked up, and I think it registered who I was, because he started to turn red.

"What are you doing here?"

"Taking a walk."

"Taking a walk! You can't take a walk here. It's private property!"

"I didn't see any signs."

"So what? I told you the other day, this land is federally protected!"

"I'm not doing anything wrong."

He struggled to his feet, glaring.

"You don't seem to understand: People aren't allowed here!"

"You're a person." I don't know why I said it; it just popped out.

He stopped as if I'd tripped him up. "I . . . I'm the *ranger*."

"What's your name?"

"I don't have to tell you that." He seemed flustered, and he'd turned red again. "I'm on special assignment— trout expert."

I took a deep breath. "*My* name's Shana Allen."

"Look, it's nothing personal, but the government doesn't want these fish bothered. They're supposed to be adapting, and they're not doing too bad, either. You come here, and I'll show you the fingerlings." He grabbed my shirtsleeve like I was a little kid.

"Let go."

"Come on. You only get to see this once in a lifetime."

"But you said—"

"They're in the pool, behind that rock. See how it's flowing upstream, against the current? We call that an eddy." He was pulling me and leaning on my shoulder at the same time. When I saw how badly he limped, I stopped being scared.

"I *know* that already. I've spent half my life fishing."

He glanced at me sharply. "Where?"

"In Virginia, on the Castle River."

He shook his head, as if the Castle was no good. Then he crouched down and patted the ground beside him. "Here."

"I don't want to."

"Then you won't see," he said crossly.

He took a plastic bag out of the pocket of his uniform, poured something into his palm, and flung it on the surface of the water. Right away three tiny fish jumped. He turned. "What did I tell you?"

I nodded, but he must have guessed I didn't know what they were, because he went on: "Fingerlings—two browns and a rainbow."

"What did you throw them?"

"Caddis larvae. I raise it for them—got a rain barrel on the side of my house. They love it."

"Is it good for bait, too?"

"I'm raising trout, not giving them away."

I thought of the fishing rod in the corner, but of course I didn't mention that. He went on: "This is a high-level assignment. You're not to mention my work to anyone, understand?"

I nodded. I guess I said what came next to knock the wind out of his sails. "We got our cat."

"What cat?"

"Felix." The name came out like I'd known it all along. "Our old orange tom."

He stared right at me. Something flashed in his watery

blue eyes, and I thought: He's measuring me up. Then he shouted, "No cats allowed near the river! If you don't keep that cat shut up, I'll issue a citation!"

I took a step back.

"I showed you the fingerlings. You know what's at stake."

"He doesn't like fish," I lied.

"There's a bluebird nesting in my yard. They almost died out, like the trout. I'm authorized to do what I have to to protect them. I have the gun!"

I left him shouting. I climbed partway up the ridge and sat for a while, to see if I could figure him out. I watched him pacing back and forth along the bank, scowling and muttering. Then he disappeared up the path. I was about to leave when he came back in his canoe. He swung it around so he was facing upstream, then slid from one side of the river to the other. He glided partway back and pushed the bow of the boat into the current. It stood still, letting the water foam around it. Then with a flick of the paddle he turned it sideways and shot into the little eddy below the rocks. He got out, took another plastic tube out of his pocket, and dipped it in the river. He threw out more larvae and wrote down what happened. Afterward he paddled back into the current and pivoted the boat so that it plummeted downstream. Before he left, he looked up as if he knew exactly where I was.

• • •

The cat was under Cody's bed, and it wouldn't come out. He'd shoved a can of tuna under there, but maybe Felix had heard what I told the ranger, because he wouldn't touch it. He howled as if we ought to know better.

"Felix?" Cody frowned. "Is he the cat from Uncle Mike's cartoons?"

Uncle Mike watched old cartoon shows each Saturday morning. He'd taught me Felix's theme song when I was little. I sang it for Cody. He nodded. "I could use a bag of tricks myself."

"Felix?" I held out my palm, and he slapped it. We didn't worry much about what Mama would say. We knew she'd let us keep Felix at the cabin, and we had no plans beyond the end of summer anyway. I told Cody I'd run into the ranger, and what he'd said. "Afterward he came back in the canoe. I've never seen anyone handle a boat like him. He's better than Eddie Brent."

"Better than Eddie?" Cody didn't believe me, I could tell. Eddie was a kid from Warrensburg who'd become a raft guide in the Cheat River Canyon. Every year someone dies in the rapids there. Cody shook his head. "You're nuts, Sha."

"Uh-uh. He can turn that boat on a dime, even in the middle of the current."

Cody changed the subject. "Why'd you tell him about the cat?"

"I didn't really think it through. I guess I wanted to shock him. He's just so . . . arrogant."

"He didn't say Felix was his, did he?"

"No. It's more like he has a right to do whatever he wants."

"He acts like he owns the river," Cody said.

We told Mama we'd found the cat in the woods—lie number who-knows-what for us, and her smiling and calling the cat and not paying much attention to the story because she had news too: They'd set a date for the accounting exam she'd have to take to get her promotion. "It's August twelfth," she said, stroking Felix. "I've got a lot of studying to do." She hated how thin he was. "We'll take him to the vet this weekend," she said. She didn't even mention the fall.

Eight

Saturday we drove to Laglade, carrying Felix in a cardboard box. Mama and Cody took him to the vet while I hung around the town house, watching TV and looking at the mail. There was nothing from Daddy, but a course list had come from Laglade High School, where I could have been enrolled come September. I thumbed through it, thinking I'd be back in Warrensburg by then. Still, I couldn't help noticing the electives they offered: not only creative writing, but photography, ecology, history of ideas, and a whole course of Shakespeare plays. Where Warrensburg had Latin and Spanish, Laglade offered those and French, Russian, and Japanese. In your junior or senior year you could go abroad, or you could take all advanced-placement courses if your grade-point average was high enough. That saved you money if you went to college, which most of the graduates did—eighty-four percent, the letter said. They had counselors who could help you get financial aid, too. I made a mental note to ask if Warrensburg High had them.

Later I took a walk and mailed my letter to Daddy. Laglade was hot, because of all the asphalt, and the car fumes stayed low in the air, so you felt like you were choking from pollution. I could hear the kids screaming at the pool from a mile away. I went past the chain-link fence, noticing a couple of girls my age. Just as I'd suspected, they had real figures and bathing suits that showed them off. They were reading magazines and chatting, while a horde of little boys ran around throwing wet towels. Nobody recognized me, and I was glad.

I went home, turned on the central air, and poured myself an iced tea. With my feet resting on the polished coffee-table, I felt like someone's guest. Then the phone rang. I expected a wrong number, but instead Uncle Mike boomed into the receiver: "Shana, you catch any fish?"

"Just a little sucker."

"Daag, I thought you and Cody could do better than that."

"The river's different." Uncle Mike made me smile without trying. "It's small and rocky, and it's got trout in it."

"You ain't gonna be outsmarted by trout, are you?"

"I hope not."

"Where's your mama? She said she'd be around today."

"She and Cody took our cat to the vet." I told him our story about Felix.

"Girl, you're telling some tales," he said at the end.

My face got red. "I'm not, either."

"Listen, tell Dot to call me, all right, sweet-pea? And Shana—"

"What?"

"The other girls are asking for you. I miss you kids myself. And I love you, too."

My eyes filled up; I couldn't help it. Mama and Cody came in just as I was hanging up the phone. Cody was full of news about the cat.

"Felix has scars from lots of fights. Even the vet says he's one mean cat."

"How come?"

"He tried to scratch him. I had to hold Felix still."

"He would have let me." I said it just to rile Cody.

"No, he likes me better. He's my pal." Cody rolled the cat on his back and scratched his belly. Felix grabbed his arm, but his claws were pulled in.

"Uncle Mike called." I told them our conversation, and Mama called him back right then. Cody and I played with Felix. If you pulled a string, he'd hide and jump it. In the background Mama said, "I haven't heard anything." "Is that so?" she said later. I could tell Mike was asking when we'd come to see him; but Mama didn't say. "You come up here, Mike. I'm having a barbeque at the cabin for everybody in the office in a week or so. Come on then. They'd like to meet you."

Mama laughed. "Just get on up here. If you don't trust the truck, I'll meet you at the bus station."

"Is he coming?" I asked when she hung up. She made a face.

"He's got more excuses than a dog has fleas."

"I miss him," I said suddenly. "And Daddy, too."

"Oh, Shana." Mama put her arms around me.

"Why can't things go back the way they were?"

Mama shook her head as if she didn't know, but when she walked away, I saw her face was tight, like a mask.

On the way back to the cabin we stopped and bought supplies: food, flashing and tar and nails, a flat of impatiens to plant by the cabin door. I got a couple of paperbacks: *Bleak House* and *A Guide to Pennsylvania's Trees and Flowers*. Cody got *Fishing for Trout* and *Rascal*, which he'd read before.

It was dusk when we hiked in. Mama cooked spaghetti while Cody made extra trips to bring back all our stuff. I lit the lantern and set it on the table. Felix circled Mama's legs, crying. "He's hungry," I said, but when I set the cat chow on the floor, he looked the other way.

"He wants Cody, I guess," Mama said.

"That's not fair. How come he likes Cody best?"

She shrugged. "Love doesn't know fair."

"What do you mean?" I asked; but she shook her head and didn't answer.

Sunday we spent the day together, just the three of us. In the morning we worked: Mama cut the flashing, Cody nailed it in, and the two of them painted pitch around the edges, then over the seams in the tar paper where the roof had leaked, Cody cleaned out the gutters while Mama and I made a bird feeder out of a slab of wood and hung it up where Felix couldn't reach.

Later I lay out on the rocks by the river and read. Mama was still working; she likes that, I think: Back home she rarely sat down, except at night. When I came up, I saw the flower garden was laid out with pretty stones, and the house smelled like pickles. Mama had made the brine and put it in a crock. She planned to bring back cucumbers the next evening. Granddaddy made pickles too. We kids used to go with him to the root cellar to check them every day. Sometimes he'd add a hot pepper or some dill on our say-so. When he finally brought the crock up, we'd have a special dinner: ham and potato salad and homemade cheese rolls, and all the pickles you could eat. We canned what was left, for winter, but they're never quite as good. I wondered if Daddy missed pickles.

That night I set the table and lit the lamp. We had macaroni with grated cheese on top, and sliced tomatoes.

Cody scorns tomatoes he didn't grow himself, but these, which came from Amish farmers off the highway, were almost as good as his. Afterward there was a shoofly pie from the same stand. We polished the whole thing off and squabbled over the crumbs. Mama's face was soft in the lamplight—pretty, I thought suddenly. What did she look like when she was thirteen? I wanted to ask, but it was safer to keep to the present, letting the past and the coming autumn stay suspended in some other place.

Monday morning Cody bugged me to go fishing. He'd read in the trout book that worms and corn are good bait on spinning tackle, and he'd managed to find a few red wigglers under rocks by the cabin foundation. He'd changed his hook size, too: down to a ten, which is tiny compared to what we're used to. The book said trout are smarter than normal fish. I wondered about that, but Cody was impatient when I brought it up: "Are you coming or not?"

"No, there's something else I want to do."

He made a face.

"Stay away from the ranger," I said.

I read for a while and then started my journal. I described the Leanna and its banks, naming some of the trees and making sketches of the ones I couldn't find in the nature guide. There were birds I'd never seen either, and I promised myself I'd learn their names over the summer. Then I told about how we'd ended up here. Writing about Daddy was hard, but later I felt relieved, as if I'd had the chance to talk to a good friend. Afterward I found raspberries on the other side of the river. I picked my fill, then waded back through the current. Cody returned with big news: He'd caught two good-sized smallmouth. He'd let them go, but it made me nervous anyway: "The ranger thinks those fish belong to him," I said.

"I was way downstream—he doesn't go that far."

"How do you know?"

"We'd see him paddle past the cabin."

I nodded, but inside I felt Cody was bound for trouble.

The week and the weekend after flew by. One day, trailing Felix through a thicket of rhododendron by the river, I came upon a hidden spot perfect for reading and writing. Where the bushes ended, an overhanging stone formed a shallow cave with a sandy floor. On sunny days I could sit on the rock ledge outside and dangle my legs in the water, but the cave sheltered me from wind and rain. I found a piece of driftwood for a shelf, and kept my books and journal there, along with a towel and a sweatshirt for cool evenings. I didn't tell Cody, and if he wondered where I was, he didn't ask.

Mama didn't either. She was busy planning the cookout for her friends the next Sunday. We helped her get the place ready, trimming the brush on the trail down the ridge and gathering wood for an outdoor fire. We even got in the river and pulled away some rocks to make a shallow pool for the little kids. Mama had invited everyone in the office and a traveling supervisor, too. Cody shook his head. "Do you think they'll bring their alligator pocketbooks?"

"Barb used to camp here when her own kids were small," Mama reminded him. "She knows what it's like, and we've told the others."

"They won't like it," Cody said. "There's snakes, and poison ivy, and you have to leave your car back near the road."

"You just don't want to share the place," I said. I thought of the ranger.

"I haven't had a party since your granddaddy's birthday, when he was seventy." Mama pushed the hair back from her face. "Then I had Mike and Charlie to help me. Ralph Emmet butchered a hog, and they dug a pit to roast it in."

"He had a big cake, didn't he?" Cody rubbed Felix between the ears. "That's the thing I remember, seeing it and hoping I'd have a cake like that when I got old."

Mama laughed. "Alma made that cake. She always loved Daddy, because he snuck her on the train a couple times when they were young—took her up to Washington and all the way down to Atlanta, so she claimed."

"Did he take you and Mike, too?"

"No, he was stricter with us kids than he was with you all. We had to stay home and help with the place."

"He didn't take you even once?" Cody turned his head from the window.

"Not once." Mama's face clouded just a little.

"Did you want to go?"

"Sure I did. But back then people didn't pay much attention to what children wanted. You did what you had to just to live. Daddy was a teenager during the Depression. His family lost their farm, and they had to camp out all winter by the river. So we were always ready for hard times: We kept the garden, and he wouldn't let Mother sell the cow or chickens even when they built the town road past the house. 'We'll have milk and eggs and potatoes no matter what,' he'd say. But when the other kids walked by and saw that cow staked in the front yard, I felt like hiding my head for shame."

"Did Uncle Mike, too?"

"No, he just laughed it off." She smiled, remembering. "He'd call out to the kids, 'Ya'll want to pat my cow? You can even milk her, if you'd like.' I was so embarrassed, I'd run ahead and pretend I hadn't heard."

"Maybe Daddy walked by," I said. "He might have walked right by and you didn't know."

"Daddy grew up on the other side of town," Mama

said. "His folks weren't much better off than us. The new shoes he got for school had to make it all the way to summer, when he could go barefoot."

I remembered Daddy's old work boots, the steel toes scraped bare of color. He laced them last thing every morning before he left the house. I wondered if he'd wanted new shoes, shoes we couldn't afford to buy.

Nine

The party turned out well. I met the people Mama had been talking about: Barb and her boyfriend, Ed; Julie; Rita and Fred; Philip the supervisor; Marilyn, Debbie, and Bob. Barb I liked especially, 'cause she'd sent me clothes for school and helped us get the cabin. She was a short round woman who was so warm you felt you'd known her a long time. She made herself at home and started serving up cole slaw and potato salad, which she'd brought in ice-cream tubs. She cut Cody a slice of cherry pie for an appetizer. She wasn't afraid of his silence, either. "I hear you haven't exactly fallen in love with Laglade," she teased, and he smiled despite himself.

There was no one our age. Barb's kids hung at the mall on weekends, and Marilyn's girls were only one and three. I helped look after them down by the river. They splashed and giggled and didn't want to come out of the water. I found a green-backed frog to lure them up the bank. Marilyn wrapped them in towels and put the baby to her breast to feed. I turned red, but Philip, an older man who was sitting with us, chatted on as if nothing special was happening. He was wearing brand-new jeans, and his leather shoes didn't look right for the outdoors. He saw me looking at them.

"You can tell I'm a city slicker," he said. "I told Dot I'd like to have you three come to Baltimore to eat with me. I love to cook, and it would be fun to show you the sights."

"Do you live right in the city?" I asked. The TV news always talked about people being murdered there.

"Yes, I've lived there all my life, and I love it." Philip smiled at me as if he could read my mind. "My apartment overlooks Mount Vernon Place. There's a Thai restaurant on the first floor, so I get to smell their food every time I open my windows."

"Food from Thailand?" I wasn't even sure where Thailand was.

"Pad Thai, green curry, chicken with lemon grass—I know their menu by heart. And next door there's a club where my neighbor plays jazz on weekend nights."

"Doesn't that keep you awake?" I thought of the sounds of the gorge, the river murmuring and the tree frogs' calls. They seemed more soothing than music. But Philip shook his head.

"When I visited my daughter in the country, I had a hard time sleeping in the quiet and the dark."

Marilyn's baby slurped her milk. You could hear her swallow: *gulp, gulp, gulp.*

"I like to hear the train whistle blow, before I fall asleep," Marilyn said. "Sometimes I lie awake waiting for it."

"Ma, I'm hungry!" Little Laura pulled her arm.

Philip held out his hand, and she took it. He extended the other one to me. "Let's go feed Laura."

I took it for a second, then pretended I had to tie my shoe. "I'll be up in a minute," I said. My face burned, and I ducked my head away so they wouldn't see. I'm not holding hands like a little kid, I thought. Still, seeing Laura scrambling up the path so happily in front of him, I wished I could.

Before the cookout ended we had ice cream with fresh raspberries on top. People were talking and laughing. Cody'd slipped away. Somebody'd brought a tape player and some tapes, old-fashioned ones like Glen Miller and Benny Goodman, and a couple of women were showing each other how to dance in the clear space outside the cabin door. Mama tried, too, first with Barb, then Philip. In the middle of the song she threw her arms up in the air and burst out laughing: "I'm hopeless."

"You were getting it, Dot," Barb said. "I was watching your feet, and you had it right."

"They have fall classes at the community center," Marilyn said. "I was thinking of signing up. Why don't we do it together?"

Mama hesitated: You could see her mind going back and forth between the pleasure of the idea and our plans to go back home. She smiled. I spoke up for her. "We'll probably be gone by then."

We walked them out, carrying Marilyn's sleeping kids and the bowls and platters the food had come in. By the parked cars people hugged Mama and said how much fun they'd had. We stood together, she and I, as the headlights disappeared into the twilight. Fireflies lit our way down the trail. We sat out front on a couple of folding chairs someone had forgotten to take. Dark settled in the gorge, flowing softly down the ridges.

"Did you like them?" Mama asked.

"They seem nice." Something pulled at me, making me say less than I should have.

"Barb's treated me like a sister—the sister I never had." Mama smiled at me. "And Marilyn, Julie, Philip; all the same."

"Philip's old," I said. "I guess he's so old his wife is dead."

Mama shook her head. "He's divorced. He used to be an alcoholic, and his wife left him because he couldn't stop drinking. Since then he's pulled himself together."

"What happened with Barb?"

"You mean her divorce?" Mama looked over at me. I nodded.

"She never told me the whole story. She started, but it's still so painful she can hardly talk about it."

"Maybe they should have gotten back together—Philip and his wife, too. Now they might be happy."

"I don't think it's that simple," Mama said.

"It's always worth one more try—that's what this counselor on TV said."

"Sometimes you can't try anymore," Mama said. "You're just worn out."

Cody came in late, picking up Felix and slinging him around his neck. Mama fussed at him for leaving the party, but you could tell her heart wasn't in it. He told me he'd gone down to the river to sit. Later he beckoned me outside. We went back beside the spring.

"I was about to come back when the ranger came down the river in his boat," he said.

"What happened?"

"I hid behind a rock. I was afraid he'd hear the music from the party—you know how sound carries on the water. . . . Then he *did* hear it. He jerked upright, spun the canoe into an eddy, and sat there listening. I was trying to figure out how to stop him when he took off upstream."

"Upstream?"

Cody nodded. "You were right about the way he handles the canoe—he's the best I've seen. He leap-frogged from eddy to eddy like the current didn't exist." He paused. "I waited around a while, thinking he might be back with one of those citations, or his gun, but he never came."

"That's weird."

"I know." He shrugged and rolled his eyes. "How was the rest of the party?"

"Good. They're nice people, all of them. Only I wish Mama didn't like them so much."

"How come?"

"What I said before—she won't want to go back."

Cody sighed. Wisps of his long hair glinted in the moonlight. "September's a ways off."

"When Daddy comes back from New York . . ."

He looked startled. "What'd you say?"

I faltered just a second. "I got a letter."

"You what? When?"

He was mad. I put my hand out toward him, but he knocked it away.

"I was going to tell you—"

"Liar!"

"Cody, I was. I was trying to figure out the right time."

"You haven't even told Mama—I'll tell her," he said fiercely, but I caught hold of his arm and pulled him back.

"We have to do this right. We could end up in Laglade for good."

"You can't keep that from her!"

"I'm not going to!"

He clenched his fists, unclenched them, looked at the backs of his hands. His mouth was a tight line. "Why'd he write *you*, anyway?"

"He knew you'd be mad. He must have reckoned I'd forgive him."

"He doesn't deserve it."

"That's what I mean."

"I'll call him," Cody said. "Did he send a number?"

"No, just an address."

"Then I'll write."

"Cody . . ."

"He doesn't belong to you, Shana. Just 'cause you shared this little secret—"

"Calm down!"

"Shut up!" Cody said, and he stalked off into the dark.

When I went inside, Mama was in bed behind the curtain. She sounded half asleep: "You and Cody go on to bed; it's late."

But I couldn't sleep. Felix prowled in and out of the room, wanting Cody, and I wondered where he'd gone. No wonder I didn't tell him things, the way he'd exploded, then run off. I wondered if he'd tell Mama about the letter before I got the chance.

• • •

When I woke up he was back, wrapped tight as a mummy in one of Gram's threadbare quilts. I heard Mama rattle around the big room, getting ready to leave for work. Before she left she peeked in, but I closed my eyes as if I were asleep.

Later I went down to my secret place beside the river. I wrote in my journal about the party, and the fight I'd had with Cody. A blue jay shrieked as if he didn't want me there. I put him on paper too, trying to capture the harshness of his cries. Then Felix appeared, and I realized it wasn't me the jay was screeching at after all. "I thought you'd stay with Cody," I murmured, but maybe Felix could tell I was upset, because he rubbed against me, just once, before he disappeared into the thicket. "Don't go upstream," I called after him.

I wrote to Daddy, telling him about the party and how Mama seemed to like it here. *Come back, before it's too late!* I put. I told him I'd let Cody know about his letter, and that he should expect one in return—not a nice one, either. Daddy had always been good at listening to Cody, had known he didn't mean everything he said. "Better for him to get it out than keep it trapped inside," he said. "That can make you crazy."

"But why does he have to be so mean?"

"Those are words on the way to something else. In the long run no one's more loyal than Cody."

Not you? Or Mama? But those questions were silent, so Daddy didn't have the chance to answer them.

When I got back to the cabin, Cody was sitting on the bench with his face over a basin of water. He dunked himself, then shook like a dog.

"Here's Daddy's address." I handed it over.

He looked at it, then up. "Did you tell Mama?"

"I will tonight."

He didn't say anything.

"When you write him, try to be nice," I said.

"Don't tell me what to do, Sha."

"I'm not, really. It's just that . . ." I broke off when he glared.

"If you don't tell Mama, I will," he said coldly.

Later we made up. We put on old sneakers and half-waded, half-swam down the river. We floated on our backs where it flattened out, splashing like little kids. In the narrow spots we kicked and jostled, each of us trying to slide through the rapids first. Once Cody won and ended up piling into a big rock. The river's so full of twists, you have to watch it every minute—even the deep pools have jumbles of boulders on the bottom. "This is the kind of place people drown," Cody said. "They get one foot wedged between rocks. The current pulls them down, and they can't get up again."

"That's morbid."

"It's true. Eddie told me. As long as you keep your legs up and float downstream, you're all right. It's getting your foot caught that will do you in."

"I'll remember that," I said, letting the toes of my old sneakers poke up through the current in front of me.

"Fish don't have feet. That's why they never drown."

"Wisdom of Cody," I told the river. "Listen up now."

"Birds don't drown either. They have oily feathers, so they pop up to the surface like corks."

"They'll get zits," I said.

"Better zits than drowned."

"What's the worst way to die?" Cody asked suddenly. He'd turned serious.

"I don't know. I never thought about it."

"What kind of cancer did Granddaddy have?"

I had to think back. "Lots of kinds, I guess, because he didn't go to the doctor till he was real sick. They didn't even bother to give him treatments."

"Why'd he go to the hospital, then? Why didn't he stay home?"

"Nobody was there. We were in school, and Daddy was working at Grove Hill."

"Still . . . don't you think he'd rather've been with us?"

"I never thought about it."

"You ought to, if you want to be a writer. They're

supposed to *contemplate*." He pronounced it slowly, as if the word tasted good in his mouth.

"I'll start tomorrow."

"Mind you do, then." He nudged my sneaker with his foot, trying to spin me back so he could go through the tongue of current and over the drop before me.

It was late afternoon when we left the river. Where we got out, the water flowed fast and deep. "Could be big rapids farther down," Cody said.

"The ranger knows. He's got survey maps on his walls."

"I wish we had one."

"Maybe he has extra."

"For us? Ha!"

"He did talk to me that time, about the trout."

"That was before he knew we had Felix."

"If he'd been mad about that, he'd have come after us."

Cody thought about that. "Maybe he was glad to be rid of him. Felix can howl. He probably kept him awake at night."

"I think he's lonely. With the trout, it was like he had to tell someone the good news."

"Dream on, Shana. He's crazy as a loon. It's a wonder he hasn't been fired."

"I might go by his cabin anyway."

"Don't."

"I'd just leave him a note . . . or maybe some raspberries. He's in such bad shape, I doubt he could walk down to pick them. Did you notice how he limps?"

Cody nodded.

"His face is odd too—kind of crooked. The two sides don't quite fit together."

"I think you should stay away," Cody said.

Mama was home when we got back to the cabin, which was bad, because we were supposed to be there in time to cook supper. She didn't seem mad, though; she'd been studying, and she said we'd eat leftovers from the picnic. Cody clammed up and stared at me, waiting to see when I'd tell about the letter, so after I set the table I plunged in.

"I've been meaning to tell you, I got a letter from Daddy," I said.

Mama was silent for a minute. It was like she was composing her response. "I knew a letter had been sent," she said. "Mrs. Grubb at the post office recognized Charlie's handwriting, and told Mike. It wasn't her business, but that's how things are in Warrensburg."

"He's in New York City, studying art and working as a security guard. He said he misses us a lot." I stumbled on. "I wrote him back, saying you'd been transferred to Laglade and we'd ended up here at the cabin." My face burned, but Mama didn't interrupt or try to help me out. "I told him to come back so we can be a family again," I finished lamely. To my left I saw Cody standing like a statue, small and pale.

"I'm glad you told me about the letter," Mama said softly. "But it was sent to you. If you get more, you can tell me or not, as you like."

"Do you want the address?"

"Yes." Mama nodded. I started to go into the bedroom to get it, but she caught my arm. "Listen, Shana," she said. "Families change, just like people."

I was afraid to ask what she meant. I glanced at Cody, but he was staring out the window.

"He'll be back," I murmured. It was something I used to tell myself when I was little and Daddy was off trucking. He wouldn't be around to kiss me good night or tell me a story, but Granddaddy or Mama would help me count the days until his rig came flying down our road and pulled into the field beside the house. I was usually out there before he had the chance to open the cab and call that he was home. I'd climb up, sit in his lap, and pull the horn just to make sure the world knew he was back. Mama would come out, if she was home from work, and Granddaddy and Cody would wander up from the garden or the spring. If he'd been away long, we'd have a celebration: chocolate milk and cookies. Mama was always glad to see him, too: They hugged, back then, and sometimes he took her face in his hands and kissed it like it was something he wanted to hold on to for a long, long time.

Ten

I stuck to my plan about the ranger. I picked two quarts of raspberries and took one up to his cabin in a plastic box. I went in the middle of the day, when I thought he'd be out working, but as I approached I saw his canoe on the bank and not long after he shouted at me from the side of the house, where he stood holding a hoe: "Hey, girl! You stop right there!"

"I brought you some raspberries!" I called, but he was already limping toward me, scowling fiercely.

"What the hell do you think—"

"I brought you these," I said, holding out the box. "Do you like them?"

His mouth fell open and he looked taken aback, as if no one ever gave him anything.

"Of course I like them! Why wouldn't I?"

He snatched the box like it was his from the start. I turned and left. I looked back once and he was standing there staring as if he couldn't believe his eyes.

I hadn't expected anything different, I told myself, but I was ticked off anyway, and I thought I wouldn't go back.

I don't know why I did. Trouble's been a magnet for Cody, not me; but our roles were changing. After Mama left in the morning, Cody would start fussing.

"Shana, you aren't going to mess with that old man today, are you?"

"Don't know what I'll do," I'd say, kind of flip. "What's it to you?"

"What if he chases you up here and sees Felix?"

"That cat won't let the ranger within a hundred feet of him. Soon as he hears him, he'll take off."

"Not Felix." That got Cody's goat. "He's not scared of nobody."

"Not like you, huh?"

He crossed his arms and looked in the other direction. "You're turning, Shana."

"What are you talking about?"

"Turning bad. Since Daddy left you've gotten hard-headed. It's all got to be your way—you won't listen to anything else."

"I do too listen!" I could feel the blood rise to my face. "I've been listening to you all my life!"

"Maybe I'm not perfect." Cody's voice was measured. "Specially back in Laglade. But since I've been up here, I've been trying. And what I hear from you is 'I'll do whatever I want.' Or else it's 'Leave me alone, I want to write.'"

For a minute I couldn't think of what to say. The writing part was true, and hard to explain. All I knew for sure was that the pages in the journal couldn't pass judgment on what I had to say. But Cody wasn't done.

"You're starting to remind me of Daddy," he said. "You think your journal's more important than real people—even your own family."

"I don't! I was just trying to sort things out, and the writing seemed to help."

"You've hardly been fishing," Cody said.

"I'll go tomorrow—I promise."

He nodded, and we let it go at that.

I went back to the ranger's. Something about the old man was drawing me there, I don't know what. This time I went in the morning, carrying some leftover potato salad and a couple of our fresh pickles. He was sitting at his cluttered table. When I knocked on the door, he was so startled he practically fell out of his chair. "Who is it? What do you want?" he hollered. Then he saw it was me.

"You again!" He didn't look friendly.

"I brought you more food—potato salad, and these pickles. We made them ourselves."

He stared at the containers in my arms, then reached out and took them. His hands shook.

"You can give me back the other box—the one I brought the berries in."

"The berries—I liked those." He nodded. "There's something else I need too."

"What?"

"Some powdered milk, and more flour. I'm almost out of flour." He put the food in an old refrigerator—the kind that's rounded on top. It didn't have much in it—there were some vegetables from his garden, and a few cans and bottles. The box I'd brought the berries in was sitting on the drain board. There was a bowl of brown soap beside it—the kind that gets soft and gloppy when it's wet.

"Flour and powdered milk—I'll write it down for you," the ranger said. He limped over to the table and cleared a space among the plants and dirty cups. He had to steady one hand with the other so he could write. He saw me watching that. "There's nothing wrong with me," he said angrily.

"I didn't say there was."

"You were looking at my hands." He thrust the paper at me. "Here."

"I'll get these soon as I can. I don't have a car." I

hurried on. "My brother and I wondered if we could borrow a map."

"What kind of map?"

"That kind." I pointed to one of the survey maps on the wall.

"You have to get those from the federal government," he said brusquely. "You *order* them."

"Could I just look at it, then?"

"For a minute." He acted like it was the world's biggest favor.

The map was hard to read. The few roads had no route numbers, and the banks of the Leanna were marked with wavy lines and red dots. Someone had drawn heavy black lines through the south section of the river. DANGER! the scrawling print beside it said. I tried to figure out where our cabin was, and the ranger's. He got a pair of heavy glasses off the table and looked through the bottoms of the lenses.

"Here." He rested his thumb on one of the dots.

"Is that your cabin?"

"What else would it be?"

"Then where's ours?" I ran my finger along the curve of the river. I figured that the brown lines marked the gorge—they were close where it was steep, farther apart where the land rose gradually. I found a dot set to the south of the ranger's. "This must be it."

"George Cosgrove's place." He said the name as if it

were a curse. "I told him to put in a septic when he built it. Now he's got people there for the summer."

"That's Cody and me! We're not doing anything wrong, either."

"Come fall, that cabin'll be torn down." The ranger turned back to the map, put his finger on another spot. "Over here's where I check the fingerlings. There's three kinds of trout spawning here—rainbows, browns, and palominos. Used to be they'd stock all three."

It took me a minute to stop him. "What do you mean, it'll be torn down?"

"Just what I said," he answered gruffly.

"You can't tear down someone else's house!"

"Won't be me. Federal government'll do the job."

I stared. "I don't believe that."

"Don't then." He turned his back and limped away.

I stood there for a minute, my hand still resting on the map. I took a deep breath. "I'm not bringing you the flour," I said. "You're too mean."

He didn't answer at first, so I went on: "You knew Cody wasn't going to steal your canoe, and putting that cat in a cage was wrong too. Seems like you hate everything that isn't part of your plan for the river." I was mad now. "You don't own the Leanna," I said. "You just pretend you do, to drive everyone else off."

"I didn't invite you here," he muttered.

"But you took the food I brought!"

"Course I did. I can't hardly get to the store, the way my leg's been acting. Can't even get up the hill to the car." He was looking out the window into the back garden.

"If you'd asked for help, we would have given it. Instead you're hateful. And now you claim they're going to tear down our cabin."

"It isn't yours anyway. And you've got another house—a year-round house. The cabin's just a summer place for you."

"You don't know about our house! It's in a development, and Cody and I hate it! If we had to stay there, we'd go nuts!"

For the first time that day he really looked at me. "What's wrong with it?"

"It's stuck in the middle of blocks of houses, with highways all around. There's nothing to do but go shopping or watch TV. It doesn't even have a real yard."

"Everybody wants that. What's wrong with you?"

"Nothing's wrong with us!" I spat out the words. "But we grew up in the country, by the river—"

"Come here," he interrupted, pointing out the window. His tone was gentler. Something blue flashed in the garden, and he nodded as if he were answering my question. "Bluebird. She's nesting in the box I made for her."

Seeing the pretty little thing made me remember Granddaddy, and I swallowed my anger. "We had those down home when I was little. My granddaddy showed me one. Later it left and never came back."

"Years ago they were common, like the trout. Now they're rare. If no one cares, they'll die out."

I watched for a minute. The bird with her bright wings and rust-colored belly seemed to be showing off just for us. She perched on a fence post, fluttered close, then went into the birdhouse.

"I'll show you something else," the ranger said. He opened his desk drawer, took out a rock, and held it out to me.

I examined it carefully. The surface was gray, but one side of the rectangular stone was honed to a fine edge. A picture was scratched on the flat surface. I ran my finger over it: an animal like a deer, but heavier.

"A bison." His voice was soft for the first time, but still urgent. "I found this along the river twenty years ago. It's Algonquin—they had settlements all along the Leanna. They lived off trout and freshwater salmon—and these."

"I thought buffalo lived on the Great Plains."

"They were driven there by civilization—and slaughtered. Them, the salmon, the trout, the bluebirds—all victims." The hard edge returned to his voice. "You can't trust people. They'll ruin everything, if they have the chance."

"Is that why you tried to chase us off the river?"

He nodded. I stared at him.

"Not everyone's like that," I said. "Cody and I care about the outdoors—we grew up in it. Anyway, you can't protect the river by yourself."

He glared. "I have the canoe."

"But they ought to send more rangers. Don't they know you need help?"

"I *don't* need help."

I tried to reason with him. "You said you can't go to the store. And what if you need medicine—"

"I don't *want* medicine!" He slammed his fist on the table. "Doctors are fools! The stuff they gave me made me sicker than I was before!"

"Calm down . . ."

"I can't calm down!" The ranger's face turned red, and he was shaking. "I don't have to listen to any damn doctor."

"I didn't say you did."

He shook his head wildly. "You probably hope I drop dead. But let me tell you something—I'm not kicking the bucket till I have this river in good hands. You and your brother and that cabin—you'll be long gone before I am."

"I'm leaving now!" I snatched my box off the drainboard.

"What about that flour?"

I turned, furious. "What about the map?"

He snorted, pulled open a desk drawer, and tossed

something on the table to my left. It was a brand-new survey map.

"You can borrow it for a few days," he said. "That's all."

I kept my promise to Cody. We went fishing that afternoon, down at the pool where he'd had luck before. On the way there I told him about the Indian ax. His eyes opened wide. "They lived along here?"

"That's what he claimed."

"I want to look for arrowheads."

"Me too. There must be books about where to search."

"We can go to the library Saturday, when we pick up supplies." Cody was excited. "Maybe the ranger's not so bad after all," he said.

I didn't answer, but I couldn't help remembering the threat about the cabin. I kept that to myself, thinking that in the long run I'd figure out what to do.

The fishing was good. The pool Cody'd found was lined with marsh grass, unusual for the Leanna, and a downed tree gave cover for bass. We started off with worms. Then I tried a plastic twister grub, bouncing it off the bottom and reeling in slow. A fish took the lure gently, then began to run. Line was pouring off my reel. I screamed for Cody to get the net.

"Keep your rod up—he'll jump!"

The fish broke water, shook; but the hook held, and I reeled like crazy now. Cody was knee deep in the water, one hand cupped around my line. I could see the shape of the fish dashing back and forth. My rod bent low. Then Cody scooped deep with the net and brought him up. "Nice one, Sha!" I clambered down to take a look.

The fish was sixteen inches, green and black, still fighting. I kept him in the net whlie I hooked him to the stringer. "Smallmouth." Cody ran a finger down his mottled side. "Will you let him go?"

"Nope." Cody and I'd had this talk lots of times. "He's dinner."

"Sha . . ." He looked at me pleadingly, but I was resolute. "You let yours go. It's been a long time since I've had fresh fish."

"I wouldn't have brought the net if I'd known . . ." Cody said, but I could tell he was pleased I'd caught a good one. We kept trying after that, and pulled in a couple of breakfast-sized bass, which we put back. By the time Mama got home, the fish was sizzling over the campfire, and we'd boiled squash and green beans, too.

"My goodness," she said. "A party."

"For Felix, too." Cody pointed.

Felix was prancing among the trees, the fish head in his mouth. We ate out front. Afterward Cody put his hands on his stomach and groaned with pleasure.

I couldn't help thinking how much Daddy would have loved that meal. He always said, "There's nothing better than fresh fish." I wondered what he ate up in New York. I decided to write to him again. There was so much I didn't know; so much that he was missing. It felt like if we didn't catch up soon, maybe we never would.

Eleven

*F*riday evening Mama brought the mail she'd picked
up at the town house. There was nothing from Daddy,
but Cody had a letter from his friend Pete back home,
telling about the Cubs' season and how some boys caught
a four-foot cottonmouth in a hole by the bridge where
the river cuts through town. Cody must have read that
thing five times.

The next day we went to the grocery store for supplies. I got the flour and the powdered milk with my own
money, and tucked them behind the backseat where
Mama wouldn't notice. Cody and I went to the library,
too. It was tiny, but the librarian was great. She showed
us how to do a computer search on local Indians, whom
she called Native Americans. The program showed a

couple of book titles, and we found them and checked them out. I got some poetry books, a bird guide, and another novel.

That evening we begged Mama to let us camp by the river. She hemmed and hawed, but in the long run she couldn't think of a good excuse, so we carried our blankets and quilts down to a flat spot not too far from the cabin. We built a fire on a rock jutting into the water. Cody threw on some hemlock branches, and the sparks flew. "Fireworks!" he shouted. He gathered more. The little green needles fizzled and popped. Then he came back with a whole armful.

"Cody! That's too many!" It was just like him to get carried away, after we'd promised Mama we'd be careful.

"It's not!" He threw them all on. Sparks shot everywhere. I grabbed our bedding and yanked it back. Beyond the fire, like a backdrop, fireflies spotted the dark. The river gleamed under flickering stars. We wrapped the quilts around us and watched. Then Cody fell asleep. The fire settled to a red glow, and the air turned cool and damp. I shivered, and decided to fetch a sweater before the night got colder.

I thought Mama would be asleep, but instead she sat by the lamp, a book in front of her.

"Are you studying?" I asked.

"No, I'm taking a break. I borrowed one of the poetry books you got from the library. I used to love poems when I was in high school."

"You did?" I'd hardly ever heard Mama talk about books, or high school, either.

She nodded. "I wanted to teach English back then. I still remember some of the poems I memorized. Sometimes I used to tell them to you when you were small. She recited one that started, "How do I love thee? Let me count the ways . . ." and suddenly I recalled sitting on her lap, hearing those words like a lullaby. Then I remembered another poem, about daffodils. She nodded when I mentioned it, and said it out loud. "You can see them so clear in your mind, can't you, Shana? I picture them under the willow tree near Ned Gwynn's barn."

"There's a girl in my class at Laglade who writes poems, and they're good, too." I told Mama about Catherine. "I tried to write some too. I might want to be a writer, or a poet."

"That's a good hobby, but you have to learn things that will help you get a job, like marketing, or computer programming. If I'd learned more about computers in high school, I'd have had more choice about the work I wanted."

"I'm not interested in that." I kept my tone mild, so we wouldn't get into an argument.

"If you go to college, you'll have time to study lots of things." Mama kept her voice neutral too.

"How come you didn't?"

"Didn't what?"

"Go to college." I was surprised I'd never asked. Mama seemed like the kind of person who'd get a scholarship if she wanted it. I said that.

"I did get one, to Radford," she admitted. "But I couldn't take it."

"Why not?"

She shrugged, as if it didn't really matter. "Family problems."

"What kind of problems?"

There was a stillness when Mama was deciding what to say. She pushed her hair back from her face. "Daddy wouldn't let me go."

I couldn't believe it. Granddaddy'd always talked about how Cody and I would be doctors or lawyers or engineers. "Why not?"

"It's a long story. . . ."

"I want to know!"

She sighed. "Remember how I told you Daddy worried about money, because of the Depression?" I nodded. Mama went on: "It took us years to convince him to get indoor plumbing, even though he had that good job on the railroad. Finally he saved up, and we did. Mike and I were in heaven when we got that faucet—we turned it on and off all day. Of course, my girlfriends didn't know—I hadn't told them we still used the outhouse and the pump." Mama's voice was strained.

"What happened?"

"When the bill came, it was more than what they'd said—more than we had, too. Daddy was in debt to the plumber. They took a lien on the land, just till he paid it back. He couldn't stand that. He was convinced we were going to lose the farm.

"We tried to tell him it would all work out, but he wouldn't listen. He'd planted the back fields in tobacco, but right away he signed on extra hours at the railroad. That left Mike and me to work the crop—you know my mother had a bad heart, so she couldn't do anything heavy. Just about then I got the letter from Radford."

"You turned down a scholarship to work tobacco?"

"I had no choice. I was seventeen, and Daddy forbade me to take it. He was afraid we'd lose the farm, afraid the scholarship meant he'd owe money he didn't have. Mother tried to talk to him. She said she'd sell her rings to pay the plumber's debt if he'd let me go. But it turned out they weren't worth what we owed."

"How long did it take you to make the money?"

"We did it, Mike and I, with that one crop. We broke our backs on it." Mama's voice was dark with anger. "That old tobacco—it's not just the smokers it hurts. Even when I wore gloves, the juice seeped onto my hands and wrists and burned so bad I thought I'd go crazy."

Her bitterness shocked me. "Why didn't you go to college later?"

"Once I turned eighteen, I wrote to them, but the scholarship was gone."

"That's not fair!"

She shrugged. "A couple of months later I met Charlie and we decided to get married. He was kind. My dreams were gone, but he had his, and they carried me for a long time."

I was aware of a rising in my stomach, like a good meal turned sour. "I thought Granddaddy was the nicest man who ever lived."

"By the time you were born, things were different. The debts were settled, and he'd even managed to pay off the mortgage on the house. He was at ease."

"Did you forgive him?"

"I tried," Mama said.

I stood there feeling lost. Then Mama looked up. "It's okay, Shana," she said softly. "I'm grown now, and I decide things for myself."

I started to shiver, and remembered the sweater in the bedroom. I put it on and headed out, into the dark.

Granddaddy said the spirits have voices: happy or sad, mad or lonely. That night the crickets seemed to groan in the underbrush, and the twigs snapping under my feet reminded me of broken bones. Mama had been a teenager, with her own dreams. What was it like, when a dream died? Did you cry as you watched it slip away?

I stumbled to the campsite and lay down. Cody sputtered in the dark. His breathing seemed unreliable, like a candle that might flicker and go out. Behind me the river gnashed stone on stone, washing down the ledges. When sleep came, I tumbled between bad dreams like a leaf scudding in a dangerous wind.

Twelve

I didn't tell Cody about my talk with Mama, not that morning, anyway. We cooked bacon over the fire, and I boiled water and made hot chocolate. Cody was looking through one of the Indian books. It said their camps were common along the Susquehanna and its tributaries, especially on the islands and river deltas. Cody started combing through a heap of stones along the gravel bar below our camp. I remembered the survey map, still neatly rolled in my backpack. I spread it on the quilt. After a bit he lost patience with his sorting and came up to see what I was looking at.

"You got a map!" He bent over. "Did the ranger give it to you?"

I nodded.

"Let me see."

I showed Cody the dots that stood for our cabin and the ranger's, and he figured out where we were, and where we'd floated that day we went so far downstream. "We were right above the rapids," he said. "Look here, Sha."

He pointed to a section of river seven or eight miles down. There the banks were steep, and the elevation—between three and four hundred feet—meant that the gorge was more like a canyon than a valley. An abandoned rail line ran for a couple miles upstream but veered north before the riverbed started to drop. After that there was no access until the Leanna merged with Tom's Creek, where a cluster of dots stood between the river and a gravel road. "Summer cottages," Cody said. "Barb told me there's a boat launch down there too. Most people who fish in the Leanna start there." Cody traced the river with one finger. He stopped at the canyon entrance. I knew what he was thinking.

"That's a long walk, even if you use the train bed partway, and once you get there, there's no trail."

"How do you know?"

" 'Cause trails are marked by dotted lines. See, even the path from the dirt road to our cabin is here. It's just so tiny you wouldn't notice unless you looked for it."

Cody nodded. "So once you enter the rapids, you're stuck."

"The ranger's map said 'Danger' all through there."

"I wish Eddie could come up, with his raft," Cody said. "We'd have fun."

"We don't know how to paddle in white water."

"You worry too much," Cody said.

I spent more time at the cave that week, thinking about Mama's scholarship. She'd never seemed to mind working for the phone company, though she'd always worried about money. I wondered if Daddy thought about Mama's dreams. Maybe he figured she was happy with her job; or maybe he spent so much time on his own dreams that he didn't have the energy for hers. I didn't like that thought, and I put it out of my mind as quickly as I could.

I wrote in my journal, imagining what Mama was like when she was young. Had she sat beside the river to learn the poems she loved?

I went to see the ranger, carrying the flour and powdered milk in my backpack. For once he didn't scowl when I showed up, and he took the supplies with shaking hands. He put everything in the refrigerator.

"Mice," he explained, frowning. "They think the cupboard belongs to them."

"What about mousetraps?"

He sighed. "I don't have time to get any. Sometimes I even wish I had that evil cat back."

"What evil cat?"

"The one you claim is yours." He looked at me sharply. "I wasn't fooled by that. But I figured if you wanted him, that was up to you, as long as you keep him away from the river."

"Felix isn't evil."

"He howled like the devil, that's for sure."

"Cody loves him."

"Cody . . . is that the boy?"

I nodded.

"Tell him to come up here," the old man said.

"How come?"

"I want to show him something."

"What?"

He glared. "Is it your business?"

"He's my brother. Last time you saw him, you were waving a gun."

He grunted angrily. The sound reminded me of a mangy old bear, and I almost smiled. Then I remembered his threats. "I won't bring Cody unless you tell me why."

"I want to teach him to paddle the canoe." He turned his back as soon as he said it.

"You want to teach Cody?"

"You've got ears, don't you?"

"We saw the canyon on the map. Will you teach him down there?"

He looked at me like I was a fool. "People die on

the flumes—good paddlers, not just kids. You stay away from there."

"We don't even have a boat."

"One time I caught some boys about to go through the falls on rubber rafts. The undercut rocks can shear your head clean off, and there're holes in the canyon that can pull you under and hold you there for weeks. What do you think they would have looked like when the river was through with them?"

I didn't back off. "How come you want to teach Cody?"

"If he's not interested, he doesn't need to come."

"He's afraid of you."

The ranger laughed harshly. "Tell him to look harder."

"Why?"

"Can't you do anything besides ask questions?"

"I brought the flour, didn't I?"

"Tell your brother to come" was all he said. I went back to the cabin as fast as I could.

Cody couldn't believe it. "Why does he want to teach me?"

"Don't ask me."

"Maybe it's a trap."

"What kind of trap?"

"I don't know—it just doesn't make sense."

"I'll go with you, if you want to talk to him."

"Couldn't hurt, I guess."

"We'll go tomorrow," I said.

That night, when I was alone, I pulled the picture box from under Cody's bed. At first the pictures seemed as jumbled as the changes we'd been through these last six months; but I dumped a bunch in my lap and sorted through them. The babies were hardest: bright beady eyes in bald heads, arms and legs as thick as hams. But here was Cody: I remembered the cowboy shirt and the fringe of light hair on his temples. I'd been fatter, but I smiled more than Cody even then. Mama and Mike were usually posed together: sitting on the galvanized washtub turned upside down, or clutching some terrified kitten. As they got older, their thin legs trailed out of baggy shorts, and thick, dark hair framed their shy faces. Sometimes Gram stood behind them. She died when I was three, so I'd hardly known her, but Mama said she'd grown up poor in North Carolina. She'd worked so hard raising cotton and tobacco that her heart was bad by the time she was forty. I remembered her propped up in bed, sewing, in her flowered nightdress. She kept a Mother Goose book beside her pillow to read to me. She'd hold out her arms, and I'd run to get in bed with her.

There weren't many pictures of Daddy as a child.

Two showed him sitting astride the mule teams that his father raised; in another, he was posed on the front porch of their old brick farmhouse. He was an only child, and people said his mother pampered him, but she died when he was twelve, and two years later his father's tractor turned over on a hillside, killing him, too. After that Daddy lived from family to family, helping out in exchange for board. At night he'd study, then read from an old set of encyclopedias his mother'd given him before she died. Maybe being on his own so young made him more eager to get married when he got the chance.

The wedding pictures were in a white album in Warrensburg; but I knew them by heart. When I was six, I'd planned my wedding to be just like theirs. Mama wore a long white dress and carried white roses, and Daddy, with his slicked-back hair, looked like a singer for a country band. They smiled for the camera as they cut the cake and stood in line with Mama's family. Now I tried to remember those smiles. Was Mama happy, or pretending? Did Daddy know she'd wanted something else? Was Granddaddy sorry for what he'd done?

I passed the beam of my flashlight over the pictures spread out on my bed, lighting up people whose lives I thought I knew. Here were Daddy and Granddaddy side by side with stringers of bass; Mama talking on the telephone in the front room; Uncle Mike posed beside his old truck, Bess. Cody and I stood on the running board of Daddy's rig in cowboy hats brought from a trip out west; in another picture he held us in his lap, smiling down as if we were a gift too good to be true.

I let the light play on those paper faces for a long time. Then I gathered them into the box and stuck them back under Cody's bed.

Thirteen

---

*T*he poplar leaves turned yellow and began to fall. I'd refused to look at the calendar, and I was fooled at first, and frightened, till Cody reminded me that poplars shed early. "Summer's not over till the sourgum leaves turn red."

"Maybe there aren't any sourgums here," I said.

Cody was whittling a bird from a pine block. "Then it won't end. We'll have to miss school. We'll stay till Christmas, cutting wood and hiking and paddling on the river."

I nodded. "I'm getting to like the Leanna. I'll bet it's pretty when there's snow on the hemlocks."

I expected Cody'd want to stay too, but he wavered.

"I wouldn't mind a few days with Pete and Jimmy, just to see what's new."

"Do you think they're still talking about us back home?"

He shrugged. "There was only so much to say, wasn't there?"

"Somebody said the whole thing had to do with that waitress at the restaurant—did you meet her, Cody?"

"Yeah." His face darkened, and he looked at the wood in his hands as if he hated it. "She was still there when we left."

"She was saving money to go to Italy. She never said anything about New York."

"Lighten up, will you?" Cody snapped his knife shut. "Coming to see the ranger?"

"I guess." He stood up reluctantly. I reached out fast and tickled him, and he slapped my hand away, laughing. We patted Felix good-bye and headed up the river.

Like last time, the ranger was almost civil. He was on the bank when we approached, a plastic tube in his hand. He eyed Cody sternly. "So you want to learn?"

Cody nodded.

"The first thing you do is look in my shed for a life jacket."

"I can swim." Cody's eyes snapped.

"Doesn't matter. State law says you have to have one on."

"I'll come with you," I said.

We went into the back, behind the cabin. The metal cage stood open, like we'd left it; morning glories and wild chickory made splashes of blue and pink among the bars. The garden had changed too: red geraniums bloomed beside the Swiss chard, and the greens had died in the potato patch. There was a fork sticking out of the ground there; but few holes. I wondered if the ranger was strong enough to dig potatoes. "Come on," Cody said.

The shed was cluttered with tools and scraps of wood. We had to brush spiders off the life vest that looked to be Cody's size. He zipped it, and it fit. I looked for one for me.

"Why?" he asked.

"I'll learn too."

"He would have told you if he'd wanted you."

"So?" I didn't want to admit that was true. I walked back with Cody. The old man was in the stern of the canoe.

"Get in."

Cody waded out. He balanced his weight by leaning one arm on the far side of the boat—Eddie had taught us that. The ranger seemed disappointed. He showed Cody how to hold the paddle.

"Going forward, your stroke looks like this." The old man dug the blade of the paddle into the water, and the boat shot forward so fast Cody almost lost his balance. "Try it."

Cody did. Before he finished the stroke, the ranger yelled, "You have to push harder than that. Watch me."

Again he stroked, his shoulder leading forward and down. The canoe lunged ahead.

Cody tried again. This time his paddle went so deep he had trouble finishing the stroke.

"Better—but you have to lean forward and extend your arm. Then you pull like you're parting the water with the paddle blade. Keep the stroke going till it's opposite your leg."

Cody tried five of them. He was pulling so hard, his face turned red.

"You're weak," the ranger said.

"I'm not."

"Then pull harder. Use the muscles in your trunk."

Cody tried again. The canoe pulled to the left, moved forward smoothly. The old man ruddered with his paddle to straighten them out. "That's a little better. You need to practice that—three hundred strokes a day, sitting in the stern. I'll supervise. But if I see you doing it wrong, or not working hard, you're done."

"Thanks." Cody's face was grim.

"Now I'll teach you the draw." The ranger demonstrated a technique that moved the boat from side to side. "You try."

I stopped watching then, but I could hear the ranger yelling as I wandered up to his cabin. The flowers on the side of the house looked dry. I remembered a bucket near the pump. I set it under the spout and pulled the handle: down, up down. It was so stiff, my arms ached by the time the water started running. I lugged the bucket over to the flowers and emptied it. Then I went inside to get myself a drink.

I knew I shouldn't do that, not without asking. The cabin was still cool and dark from evening; facing north and sheltered by ridges, its windows caught the late-day sun. There was a jar of water in the refrigerator, and I rinsed out a mug and drank. I couldn't help looking around. Without the ranger, the room seemed quiet and settled, a cross between a study and the messy bedroom of a little boy. Some of his uniforms hung from pegs, but a bunch of dirty ones had been tossed in a heap by the closet door. Old sneakers and boots poked out from under the bed, where the sheets looked stained and crumpled. An open dresser drawer showed a tangle of socks and underwear.

"You should wait outside," I told myself. I looked out the window and saw the canoe still on the river. I went over to the ranger's desk and poked around.

His books, mostly about trout, lay on the desktop, along with his pocket notebooks. The top drawer held a mix of papers, some rubber-banded together: fishing regulations, something from Social Security, what looked like a health-insurance bill, and a bottle of pills.

"Take three times daily for high blood pressure," the directions said. The script was dated two years ago, in the name of Henry Luck, but the bottle was almost full. *You're a snoop,* Cody's voice whispered in my ear, but I shook my head to chase it away. I turned to the table.

That was the worst: a clutter of books, half-filled cups of coffee, plates stained with egg yolk and dried baked beans. Two dented pans held water: for the flowers, I supposed, which bloomed in cracked clay pots in the middle of the mess. I picked up a book; bookmarks fluttered out like falling leaves. I gathered them up and stuck them hastily in the front.

They were coming off the water. I went out the back door and around as if I'd spent the whole time in the yard. Cody looked awful: red and walking like he hurt all over. The ranger was yakking it up behind him: "Don't forget about the left side when you practice. If you don't build your strength there, you'll be good for nothing."

Cody didn't answer.

"Same time tomorrow."

"Right."

"Wait a minute," I said. "Do you want to, Cody?"

"I can speak for myself," he said wearily, and when I started to open my mouth again, he shook his head.

At home Cody soaked in the river for a long time. Then he rolled himself in his quilt and lay on the floor. He was so tired, he could hardly talk.

"Why didn't you tell him you were worn out?"

"I don't know."

"Why's he doing this?"

"I asked him. All's he said was 'I have to.' "

"That sounds like someone told him to."

Cody shrugged.

"He lives by himself. I looked around the cabin. There's no sign anybody even comes to visit."

"He's got something wrong with his left hand. After a while he had to tape his fingers to the shaft of the paddle. He used duct tape." Cody winced.

I didn't mention the blood-pressure medicine in the drawer. I asked, "Why is he so mean?"

"I learned a lot."

"Why you? I could learn to paddle." But the truth is I'm not as strong as Cody. I'd last about three minutes practicing those strokes. I wondered if the ranger knew that.

The next day we went back. This time the old man took me aside. "I need meat and eggs," he said. "I have to keep up my strength."

"Meat and eggs cost money."

He opened a side drawer in the desk, took out a twenty-dollar bill, and handed it to me.

"I'll get them when Mama goes to the store. What kind of meat do you want?"

"I don't care—anything."

"What if she sees?"

"She better not see—I told you, this assignment is secret."

"I'll do what I can. If you're nice to my brother, I'll get more."

"I don't have time to be nice."

"That's silly—you can be nice in the same amount of time you can be mean."

He looked at me. "Not if you don't know how."

He put Cody through the mill. I couldn't stand to watch after a few minutes, so I went back to his house and sat on the front porch. His cabin was better built than ours—the edges of the logs were carefully caulked, and the mortar was pointed up where it had started to crumble. The windows were real, and were lined with wood storm windows and screens. Blue curtains and a hooked rug by the cast-iron stove, a pretty pillow in the rocking chair, a bedspread: color could have made this place nice. . . . I wondered if the ranger had been married. If he had, there was no sign of it. On the other hand, who would put up with him?

He was yelling now—at Cody.

"Can't you do anything right? I told you, *draw stroke*!"

Cody changed grips, but the ranger wasn't satisfied. "You have to pull! Put your weight behind it!"

Cody mumbled.

"I don't care how much you weigh! If you can't do better than that, you're weak!"

Later he softened. He got out of the canoe and stood on the bank, directing Cody in and out of an eddy that lay to one side of a small rapid. "Keep the boat at the same angle all the way across—paddle steady—steady now! Straighten out her bow! Now cross over and bring her around!"

Cody knelt in the middle of the canoe. At times the front end twisted in the current. Then the stern would stray, and he'd have trouble getting the boat back in line. The ranger warned him about pinning if you let the canoe swing sideways: "It'll hit a rock and fill up with water. That's a thousand pounds you never bargained on. If you get caught between the boat and a downstream rock, you can be crushed like this." He crunched his heavy boot on the riverbank.

I pulled on his arm. "We've got to go. We're supposed to make supper, and Mama gets home at six."

"Mama!" He sneered. "We can't disappoint Mama."

"If we're not on time, she'll ask where we've been." My voice was icy.

"Better get in here, Cody. Sis says you've got to go."

Cody paddled in. His face was flushed. He pulled the boat up and chained it.

"Come tomorrow, at the same time," the ranger said. "And remember the meat."

"I told you, I'll try to get it Saturday."

"Then Saturday."

"I'll do it when I can."

"You seem tired, and your face is red," Mama said to Cody later. "Are you getting sick?"

"No, it's sunburn."

"Wear a hat tomorrow," Mama said. "Or stay inside. You said you'd make frames for the plastic in those windows. The boards have been standing in the corner for two weeks."

"I'll do it this weekend."

"This weekend? What's to keep you from doing it tomorrow?"

"Nothing, really. I just had something else planned."

"What?"

"Nothing much . . ."

"I can do the windows, if Cody draws the angles for the corners," I said.

Mama looked from one of us to the other. For the first time she seemed to notice there was something odd. She took her dirty dishes to the stove and started heating the wash water. She didn't say anything, but a couple of times that evening I caught her looking at us, and I knew she was wondering what was going on.

The next day rain saved us. We stayed inside and worked on the windows, and played with Felix. I read to Cody from the Indian book, about how their camps were set up and what they ate. Then I read his favorite part of *Rascal*, which we'd read a hundred times before: where Sterling goes out in the canoe and sets the raccoon free. When I finished, Cody sighed. "Do you think that's how it really was?"

I pondered that. "I doubt it. In real life your shoelace breaks, or you have to pee in the middle of what you're doing."

Cody was using the mitre box, lining up the corners of the window frames. "Would you have let him go?"

"Who?"

"Rascal."

"I don't know. I might have built a bigger pen, so he'd be happier at home."

"What if he wasn't?"

"I would have tried things till I figured out what worked."

"What if nothing worked?"

He was making me edgy. "I don't know."

Cody squinted at the wood in his lap. "Remember Richie Bird?"

"What about him?" I turned red. Richie was a high-school junior who rode the bus with us back home. Last winter I started getting flustered whenever I was around him. But I didn't think anyone noticed, and even though he was good-looking and nice, I stayed away so I wouldn't have to face my own confusion.

"You had the hots for him," Cody said.

"Shut up! I didn't, anyway."

He shook his head in disgust. "You're pretending, Shana."

"You don't know!"

"Everybody knew!"

"Brat!" I slapped his face. Cody drew back. He broke the piece of wood in two. Then he went out, into the rain.

Fourteen

Cody and I stayed apart after that. Mama could tell we'd had a fight. She didn't ask what happened, but she did say it was hard to get along when you spent so much time together. After breakfast I'd slip down to the cave and sit. If I was still enough, the water snake that lived upstream would crawl from under its rock and hunt for minnows in the pools along the bank. Another time a sleepy-looking possum trundled through the under- brush and stared as if I were a visitor from another planet. One rainy day a huge bird dropped into the river right in front of me. He went under water, came back up, and flew away with a fish dangling from his yellow talons. The ranger said that was an osprey, and that he'd better leave his trout alone; but he smiled when he said it, as if he knew he were no match for a hawk that big.

Cody started going to the ranger's by himself. It wasn't something we agreed on; it was more like we weren't talking, and neither of us asked the other, Are you coming?

I took the old man meat and eggs. I bought them Saturday while Mama and Cody were at the hardware store. Soon as I got the chance, I took them to his cabin. He wasn't home, so I put it all in his refrigerator. Then he came in and surprised me. He looked sick: His eyes were glassy, and he wobbled like he might fall down.

"What are you doing?" he demanded.

"I brought the food."

He looked so bad I made him a platter of eggs and sausage. He ate them like he was half starved, bending his face down and shoveling the food in with his right hand. When he finished, he closed his eyes for a second. "Cody's doing all right," he said.

I didn't want to hear about Cody, but he went on: "He says you're a writer."

I was taken by surprise. "I'm just learning."

"He thinks you'll be good."

"He does?"

The ranger nodded. He kept his water supply in gallon jugs under the drainboard and in the bathroom; I poured some into a pan and set it on the stove. "What's that for?" he asked.

"The dishes."

"I can wash them," he said gruffly.

"I know you can. What I'm saying is, this time you don't have to."

We were quiet for a while. I saw the bluebird fluttering in and out of her house. The afternoon sun began to slant through the window, lighting up the table and the iron sink where I stood. The ranger nodded off in his chair. The water boiled, and I put the dirty plates in the sink with a glob of hand soap. Usually I don't like washing dishes, but the view out the window—the bluebird, the flowers, the ridge with its fringe of pine and hemlock—was soothing. Then the ranger startled and woke up. He looked around.

"Who are you? What are you doing here?"

For a second I thought he was joking. "I'm Shana— I brought the meat."

"What year is it?" He looked upset. He gripped the edge of the table.

I told him.

"You're lying." He looked down at his hands, stared at them. "I thought you were Edna, but she's gone. Gone and good riddance."

"Who's Edna?"

"Now I remember—you're the one with the brother, the one who's always asking questions."

I nodded.

"She's none of your concern." His voice was cold.

"I didn't bring her up."

"No, I don't guess you did." He wiped one hand across his face. "I've been having this trouble," he said suddenly. "Not all the time, just now and then . . . this trouble remembering." His voice quavered. I couldn't help staring.

"I know some things: I was born in 1918 in Williamsport. We lived at Forty-three Sumner Place. My mother was Rose Green and my father was William Henry Luck. I went to St. Michael's Primary School." He looked up, and his voice trailed off. "The rest comes and goes."

I'm not sure why, but I wanted to change the subject. "The bluebird's in the house you made for her," I said.

"I don't want anyone to know. . . ." He went on. "They have cages for people like me, old people who can't remember. You lie in bed and eat pablum."

"Pablum's for babies."

"It's a way of life, for them."

I stirred the dishes in the sink.

"Have you ever been afraid?" He looked right at me now. "Not just a little bit, but really afraid?"

"I don't know." I was afraid right then.

"I have." He went on, but he was staring at his hands instead of me. "The first time I went through the canyon I was that afraid. I saw the first drop coming, and I thought: 'This is it, Henry. You're going to die.'" His hands clenched and unclenched.

"I gripped the paddle. The boat slammed into a wave and started to flip. Somehow I knew to brace on the right: Maybe there was an angel watching, whispering what to do. . . . I was crying, praying to get through it. Every cell in my body wanted life. I paddled like a madman, and in the end, the river shot me out alive." He looked up now. "Beginner's luck. You get that once or twice."

I didn't move.

"After that I told myself I'd change: treat people good. For a year or so I tried. But it was too hard. I was rough leather to their silk. There was a few put up with me, just a few, and after a while they gave up too. I told myself I'd marry the river, and I did. I learned her ways, even the flumes; and I gave her children, too."

"The fingerlings . . ."

He nodded.

"I'm sick, but I'm holding on, just like I did in the canyon that first time. Old as I am, I still want life." His voice broke then.

I was afraid to speak, afraid to move. He must have know that.

"Go on," he said roughly. "Go on home."

I went back to the cabin. I wanted to talk to Cody so bad, but he wasn't there. I sat a bit with Felix, feeling the warmth underneath his fur. He purred and licked one paw. I saw where the space between his ribs had filled out over the summer. I'd grown too: There were new muscles in my arms and legs, and the beginning of roundness in my chest. I'd wanted things to go back the way they'd been, or even stay the same; but it was starting to seem like nothing stopped you growing.

I went down to the cave and got my journal. My mind was so full of the ranger I felt choked, and the words wouldn't come. I picked up a rock, then another, and flung them into the water. I thought of Cody searching for arrowheads, thought of the Algonquin families that lived along this shore hundreds of years ago. I imagined a girl my age standing as I was then, throwing stones because she was too full of feelings to do anything else.

Later—all of a sudden—I heard a poem. It came so quietly that it seemed as if it must have been there all along, like a sleeping cat that wakes, stretches, and shows itself. I wrote it down, holding my breath so that it wouldn't disappear before I got the words on paper. Later, I thought, I'll read it to somebody—maybe.

That evening Mama had something serious to say: "I'm taking the state accounting exam a week from Saturday. It's in Baltimore, and it takes four hours. I'll be gone the whole day."

She looked at us hard. "Philip has invited you to stay with him while I take the test. He plans to take you out to lunch at a restaurant near his apartment, and to see the Orioles play that afternoon." She paused. I wondered if she'd told Philip how bad Cody wanted to go to Camden Yards. He was so wild to see it, he would have gone there with the devil himself. Now he sat across from me with his mouth hanging open.

"You mean Philip has tickets to the ball game?"

She nodded.

Cody clenched his fists over his head. "Wait till Pete hears about this!"

"I'd rather stay here." The words felt thick in my throat.

Cody gaped. "Rather stay here than go to the ball game? What are you, crazy?"

"I just don't feel like going." I glared at him.

"Don't you know how hard it is to get tickets? It's impossible!"

I shrugged as if I didn't care.

"You're crazy!" Cody said.

Mama talked to me later. "I'm not sure I want you here alone, Shana. We won't get home till after dark."

I didn't answer, but I was thinking: You can't make me go. Mama asked, "What if you fell and broke your leg?"

"I'll stay around the cabin. I won't even go fishing, if you don't want me to."

She looked right at me. "I think you'd enjoy this, Shana, if you'd let yourself."

I didn't answer.

"Philip is my friend, just like Barb and Marilyn. There's nothing else between us, if you're wondering." She got mad then. "But if there were, that would be my choice, not yours."

My face burned. "Cody and I are stuck with what you want! You didn't even ask before you decided to move! We had to come along whether we wanted to or not!"

She nodded, but her lips were tight. "I made the decision I thought was best."

"Best for you! What about us?"

Mama looked away. My eyes filled up. I went into the bedroom and slammed the door. Cody was in there reading a comic, but he slipped out without looking me in the face.

That night I wrote to Daddy:

Mama has a friend in the phone company, and he's got tickets for the Orioles for Saturday. Remember how you used to say we'd go see them play? Now it's going to happen, but with someone else.

Why don't you write to us? Why don't you tell us when you're coming back?

I almost signed the letter then, but after I addressed the envelope, I decided to add another line.

I've met a ranger, and I wrote this poem.

I copied it, folded it with the letter, and stuck them both in the envelope.

Fifteen

After Mama left for work, I talked to Cody.

"Those baseball tickets are a lure, and you're the fish who's dumb enough to bite."

He looked at me blankly. "What do you mean?"

"Philip wants you—or us—to like him, because he likes Mama. And this is a sure way to get you to."

"If you think I'm going to miss that ball game, you're nuts," Cody said.

"You need to think about what it means, Cody."

He rolled his eyes. "I think Philip's trying to be nice."

"How do you know?"

"Because Mama said he's just a friend. Anyway, she can't spend her life waiting for Daddy to come back."

"It's been six months! That's only half a year!"

Cody sighed, and for a moment I thought I saw tears in his eyes. He shook his head. "I'm not missing that ball game."

"You're selfish."

"*You're* not my boss, Shana." That was all he had to say.

The next few days were awful. Cody'd told Mama yes about the day with Philip, and she was leaning toward making me go too. It didn't help that she was nervous about the test; every spare moment she was bent over a book or a sheet of figures. I felt so alone. I wanted to see the ranger, but I was afraid he'd be weak and sad, like before.

I also worried I'd find Cody there. He disappeared each morning without telling me where he was headed. When I tried asking him, he wouldn't answer. "You're supposed to let me know where you're going," I said. "That's what we agreed to do."

"You just want to bug me," Cody said.

"What if you drown? I won't know where to look for your body."

"Ask the ranger."

"He might drown too!"

Cody grinned. "You'll hear his ghost cussing me out: 'Don't you know how to paddle, boy? Call that a draw stroke? If you can't do better, I'll have to issue a citation!' "

We both laughed then, and Cody headed up the river.

Later I went up myself. I wondered if he'd still be there, but the canoe was chained and the old man was stomping around upstream, yelling at a couple of guys in a flatboat.

"You can't fish here! There's a state boat launch down the river at Tom's Creek."

One of the men said something to him.

"If you don't turn back, I'll write you a citation. I'm the ranger here, and this part of the river is federally protected. You can't fish here—you can't even walk here."

The guy answered.

"I'm not telling you again," the ranger said. "Listen to me, or face the consequences in court!"

Slowly, reluctantly, the men turned their boat and poled upstream. The ranger stood there, hands on hips, watching them go. Then he came down to the bank, clucking like an old hen. He didn't even say hello.

"They act like fishing is a right! Said they didn't see any signs! I should have asked to see their licenses. Fishing without a license carries a one-hundred-dollar fine!"

"I'm surprised we don't see more people around here."

He turned like I'd threatened him.

"There's no public access. They can go to Tom's Creek. That's where they're supposed to fish!"

We turned and walked up toward the cabin. He was mumbling under his breath as if I weren't there. Then out of the blue he asked, "Will you dig some potatoes?"

I nodded.

"Let's do it now," he said.

I've dug potatoes lots of times back home, so I know what I'm doing, but of course the ranger didn't think so. "You'll cut them up if you dig that close to the stem," he fussed. I ignored him and did what Daddy had shown me, pulling back the dried-up stalk and then digging around it till I could lift the mass of tangled roots. He had a good crop: I pulled two dozen potatoes from three plants.

"Where do you want them?"

"In the bucket. They have to be scrubbed."

I wondered if he'd ask me to do that, but he was too stubborn. He could barely prime the pump without losing his balance, and when the water finally ran into the bucket, he picked it up and swished it around as if that was all it took. He poured off a stream of mud, stared dolefully at the potatoes, then thrust the pump handle up and down until the bucket filled again. He rinsed the potatoes and dried them on his shirttail. I was poking around the garden. He had a bed of wildflowers, and there were some I'd never seen before, tall with dark-pink petals.

"What are they?"

He grunted.

"What?"

"Wild phlox!"

"They'd be pretty at our old house, next to the porch."

"Come back like weeds every year, no matter what." He shrugged as if he didn't care about them, but I could see he did, 'cause they'd been tended.

"Where'd you get the seeds?"

"I didn't. She planted them." Before I could ask more, he went into the house and slammed the door. I followed him in. Before long the pungent smell of sausage filled the room. He cut up some potatoes and threw them in with the meat. Then he cracked an egg over the whole mess. He glanced at me.

"Want one?"

"No thanks."

He poured the food onto a plate and shoveled it down. Afterward he said, "Forget about what I told you the other day."

"Okay." I'd wanted to, but suddenly I regretted it. He'd talked to me like a friend. Now his voice was harsh, like I was used to. He looked out the window as if there was something more interesting than me out there. "Winter squash is coming in."

"My daddy used to make squash pie."

"I didn't think you had one. You all talk about Mama."

It took me a minute to figure out what he meant. "He's away."

"Where?"

"New York."

"How come?"

His coolness bugged me. "What do you care?"

"I don't." He pushed his fork around his plate, then struggled to his feet. His head was bent over the sink. "Only I had a kid once."

"You did?"

He shrugged, as if it wasn't important. "She's grown now. Last I saw her, she told me to drop dead."

"What's her name?"

"Daisy . . ." He was looking out the window, but his eyes seemed far away. "I named her that."

"Was Edna your wife?"

He turned angrily. "Where'd you hear Edna?"

"You said it yourself, the other day."

"I never say that name out loud."

"You'd just waked up, remember? And you asked what year it was, and then you said—"

"All right!" he snapped. He smacked the dishes against each other so hard I thought they'd break. "You can count on people to let you down," he said.

At first I thought he meant me, and I bristled, but he went on: "Her, Daisy, your daddy . . . there's always someplace better, or somebody."

"Daddy's not like that."

He didn't look at me. "You're making excuses for him."

"I'm not! Everyone deserves a chance to follow their dreams! Look at you—you're here, with the river."

"That's different," he grunted. "They left me."

"You said you were miserable to be with!" I couldn't let up. "Daddy's nice!"

The old man stiffened, breathed deep. "I'm here listening—he's not!"

"He'll be back."

"I'll look out for him." He laughed abruptly.

"Shut up!" I would have run away, but my eyes were full of tears.

"You don't get it," he said slowly. "I'm trying to tell you what it took me years to learn."

"What's that?"

He leaned over. "Don't count on anybody."

I should have asked him then and there what he wanted with Cody. Instead I came back to our place and pulled the weeds that had sprung up in Mama's flowers. Afterward I went to the cave and wrote in my journal. I tried to imagine the ranger's daughter. What had she looked like? Did she love her father, despite everything? Or had she finally given up?

Later, back home, Cody came up the bluff. He had two fishing rods in one hand, and his old sneakers were oozing water.

153

"Catch anything?"

It was a good thing I asked. His face lit up. "A twelve-inch brown trout."

"Let's see!"

"I threw him back."

"You're making it up."

"I'm not. Got him on a spinner down near the fallen tree. He took it and ran."

"Lucky!"

So Cody had caught the first trout.

Sixteen

_P_hillip told Mama I shouldn't have to go if I didn't want to. He offered his dog Nina for protection, since I'd be alone. Mama looked sheepish when she showed up Friday with the dog in tow. We'd thought it would be a German shepherd or a Doberman, but instead a fat old bulldog came trundling down the trail behind her.

"Philip claims she barks at strangers," Mama said. Just then Cody appeared from behind the house. He stared.

"That's the ugliest dog I've ever laid eyes on."

Nina wagged her tail.

"Take her with you wherever you go," Mama told me. "Philip says she gets nervous when she's left alone."

Cody grinned. "Sounds like you'll be baby-sitting her."

"You can still change your mind, Shana. We'd be happy if you came with us."

For some reason I actually considered it. "No, thanks."

Nina whined and rubbed her head against my knee.

They got up early. I managed to tell Mama good luck before they left; but when I got back in bed, the trouble started. Felix had been outside all night. When he saw Nina, he freaked out and started spitting. She acted like she'd never seen an angry cat. Her eyes got big, and she began to howl. I grabbed her collar and pulled her into the main room. A cascade of hisses exploded behind us. Nina stared dolefully at the bedroom. Then she climbed onto Mama's cot and fell asleep.

We'd had dogs before, back home: coon dogs and mutts and a Labrador retriever named Andy. But they lived outside, in doghouses, and were mostly used for hunting, though Cody and I sometimes took them off their chains and played with them. After Granddaddy died, Mama gave the dogs away, and I can't say that I missed them much. Daddy didn't either. Though we'd told him over and over, he'd never even learned their names.

I thought about Daddy. He didn't like animals, except for horses; they were too much work, he said. He'd had to muck out stalls when he was little, and after that he hated cleaning up, even after himself. Mama'd get mad at him for leaving dishes in the sink. He said she should buy paper plates, so no one had to wash them. "What's money for, anyway?"

"Charlie . . ." Mama'd pick up a stack of envelopes, hold it in front of him. "Do you know what these are?"

"Let's go," Cody'd whisper. He hated it when they argued. We'd slip outside and climb the apple tree. If it was fall, Cody'd throw rotten apples at the wreck of the tobacco shed. He loved it when they splattered on the crumbling wood.

I shifted on the bench, scratched Nina's head. Mama'd be bent over her test now, and Cody and Philip on their way to Camden Yards. I could almost hear them laughing as they strolled the city streets. They're having fun, I thought. Nina sighed, as if she felt sad too. "Come on," I said, "we're going for a walk."

I had to coax her out and down the ridge. I knew a place where a brook came into the river over a series of waterfalls. I showed Nina a mess of Christmas ferns I'd found there. Then I decided to build a dam where the banks were close. We used to love that, when we were kids; sometimes Cody and I would spend a morning piling rocks and mud and wet leaves into a wall. But by myself, it wasn't as good as I remembered. The dam leaked, and rushing to patch it I broke my fingernail on a stone. Then I stumbled into the water and got a hotfoot. Usually I don't mind that, but I wasn't expecting it, and the wet shoe rubbed against my sock and felt like it was starting a blister. I went back to the cabin to change.

Maybe Nina was smarter than she looked, because as soon as I started toward the house, she trotted happily behind me. She scurried through the door and flung herself onto Mama's cot with a snort of relief. I fixed myself a sandwich and some Kool-Aid. I couldn't help wondering, What are Cody and Phillip doing now?

I got the idea after lunch. I was thinking about Uncle Mike, and how good it felt talking to him that day at the town house. I thought suddenly: I'll call him! Then, replacing that idea before it even took hold, came another: I'll call Daddy. He may not have a phone, my mind argued—after all, he didn't send a number. "But that was a while ago," I answered out loud. "I bet he's got one now. I'll call information in New York and get the number. I can use our card, so there won't be any reverse charges."

I wanted to leave Nina, but I was afraid to after what Mama'd said. So I pulled her up the trail. Poplar leaves fluttered around us. I came to the end and followed the road to Mrs. Burns's house. I'd met her only once, when Mama'd introduced us and explained that we could use the phone or go to her in an emergency. As soon as she opened the door, I told her, "There's nothing wrong. I was just wondering if I could make a call."

"Of course." She beckoned me in, then noticed the dog.

"Stay," I said. I closed the door.

"The telephone's here." Mrs. Burns pointed to a little table by the couch. "I'll leave you alone, for privacy." But she paused on her way out. "Are you sure everything's okay?"

"It's fine—I just want to call a friend I haven't seen for a while."

She went out then, and I got the New York City area code from information. I phoned it and asked for a new listing for Charles Allen on West Seventy-ninth Street. The operator seemed to take forever. Then a recording said the number before I realized I didn't have a pen. I'll have to remember it, I thought; and I listened one more time.

"212-555-6655," I said under my breath. My fingers trembled as I dialed and gave the billing information. Another operator put the call through. I heard the familiar clicks of phone lines connecting. Then it began to ring: *veeeeeep, veeeeeep, veeeeeep.*

He isn't home, I thought, and I almost hung up; but I wanted so bad to talk to him, so I held on one more minute. Then, amazingly, the ringing stopped, and someone said, "Hello?"

"Hello, Daddy?"

"Hello?"

I stopped, the phone still in my hand. I willed my fingers to push, and the line went dead. Mrs. Burns must have been listening in the other room, 'cause she stuck her head in. "Did you get through?"

"Yes, thanks." I put the receiver down and went outside. Nina was waiting for me, but I shoved her away and took off down the ridge. I could hear her behind me, chugging along like an old steam engine. *Hello? Hello? Hello* . . . the voice repeated. "Daddy?" I'd said, before it had even registered, so he would know I'd called, but not because I'd talked to him. The voice on the phone, soft and Southern like Daddy's, was a woman's.

I took it out on Nina. I closed her out and shouted, "Go away!" I lay on Mama's cot with the pillow over my head. If I'd been able to cut it off, maybe I would have then: to stop the thoughts and undo the phone call. Maybe I'd undo the last six months of my life. From the bedroom Felix cried piteously, but I knew he liked Cody better than me, and I yelled, "Shut up!"

I wanted to disappear. I imagined myself shrinking slowly back in time: getting smaller, smaller; back to the moment I was born and then beyond—a fetus, an embryo, an egg. If I'd had an eraser I could have erased that tiny dot and saved myself a lot of disappointment. *Don't count on anybody,* the ranger said. I hated him, too: hated him for telling me something so mean and so true.

• • •

I pretended I was sleeping when they got back. Mama came over to the bed to check on me. She put her palm on my cheek. "We're home, honey," she said softly.

Next morning Cody wouldn't shut up. "You don't know what you missed, Shana!" he babbled. "The Orioles won six to three, and we had seats along the first-base line. We could see everything!"

I didn't answer. Mama asked, "What did you do?"

"Nothing, really. How was the test?"

"Hard, but I think I did okay." She smiled at me. "Anyway, it's over. In three weeks they'll announce the scores."

"What then?"

"I'll turn them over to the phone company, with my request for promotion. They'll decide what to do."

"What if they turn you down?"

"I'll try again next year." She stirred her coffee.

"Old Mr. Weiss might be dead by then," Cody said. "You could run the office back home."

"You never know." Mama hummed to herself.

But I knew, and I wished I didn't, something about her husband, my daddy: something that felt like a punch, or a slap, or a throw so hard that the dice this game is played with might be gone for good. I had a family once, but the word is cracking into pieces. Some of them may even disappear.

Seventeen

"You could have dialed the wrong number," Cody said when I told him. "You said you didn't write it down."

"I think I recognized her voice."

"Whose voice?"

"That waitress—Paula."

Then Cody got snide—maybe because it hurt him, too. "He's there by himself—he can do what he wants, can't he?"

"Maybe he won't come back after all," I said.

Cody stared at me. I guess he knew I felt bad, 'cause he took a Milky Way out of his pocket and broke it in two. It was squishy, but I ate it anyway. When I was done, my insides still felt empty.

"What if they get a divorce?" I asked. "What about those promises?"

"What promises?"

I knew the words by heart because of the times I'd played wedding when I was little. " 'For better or worse, in sickness or health'—all that."

Cody shrugged. "I guess they lied."

We sat for a while. Felix came along, and Cody rubbed his fur the wrong way, then smoothed it back into place. "The ranger was married once," I told him. "He and his wife had a little girl. She's grown now, and she hates him."

"He can be nasty."

"Do you think he's gotten worse?"

"His yelling?"

"No, the way he limps, and how weak he seems."

"I think so. The minute we come in from paddling he sits down and falls asleep." Cody stretched. "I'm going up there in a half hour. He's going to show me how to run a Class Three rapid."

"What's Class Three?"

"Whitewater's rated one to six according to how dangerous it is. A one is easy, and a six is impossible—like Niagara Falls. Threes and fours are serious rapids."

"You might get hurt."

He shook his head. "There's a big drop, but if you flip, there's nothing down below to bang you up. That's why it's a good one to learn on."

"I want to see."

"I'll ask if you can come tomorrow."

"Why not today?"

But Cody shook his head. "I want to try it on my own."

"I don't see why I can't come," I muttered, but Cody'd made his mind up, and he didn't bother to answer.

After he left, I went to the cave, but all I could write was the word *Hello*. I filled a half page with that before I put the journal away and lay on the ledge on my stomach. I could see water striders putt-putting in the pool beside me. I wondered if there was a pattern in what they did; if they made choices: Left or right? Forward or back? Did they have minds, feelings, dreams? A chickadee noticed me from the low branches of the hemlock across the river and flew closer, staring curiously. "I'm new here," I explained. The little bird twittered as if it understood.

Later I went to the ranger's. I saw Cody on my way: He'd made it through the rapids twice, but the third time he got stuck in a reversing wave and flipped. He was soaked, but happy. "You've got to try it, Sha. It feels like flying."

"What good is flying if you get pneumonia?"

"Wait till you try it," Cody said.

I'd made up my mind not to talk about Daddy, but the ranger was so beat he couldn't pay attention anyway.

He was sitting in his desk chair with wet boots on his feet and his mouth half open. When I came in, he snapped it shut.

"Your brother's wearing me out," he mumbled. "He doesn't know when to quit."

"I saw him on my way here. He said he made it through the rapid."

"Of course he made it! He's a natural. I guessed it the first time I saw him."

I didn't argue. I cooked him a hamburger and a pan of beans, and he slurped them down. Then I helped him get his boots off and gave him a cup of tea. It must have been in that cupboard for years, it was so musty; but he didn't care. After he drank it, he sighed and closed his eyes.

"I wrote a poem," I told him.

He wheezed in his sleep, and I left him in the chair and headed home.

When I got back to the cabin, Cody had made a fire and was sleeping beside it. It was his night to make supper, but I decided to start it myself. That meant I got to pick the meal, and I chose spaghetti and garlic bread. The whole time I was working, I kept thinking of that phone call. What if I hadn't hung up? Then I'd know what was going on, instead of imagining the worst. What a jerk I was, to panic like that! Like Cody said, I didn't even know if I'd got the right number.

• • •

That night the three of us went fishing. We bundled up in sweaters and windbreakers and climbed down to stand by a quieter stretch of the river. Maybe because we'd come on impulse, we'd brought only one rod and a few lures. We took turns casting over the water and reeling in slow. Bats dove for insects in the dusk, and the dark ridges on both sides of the Leanna framed the fading light. Cody talked about the ball park, and Philip's apartment.

"You can hear his neighbor Marvin practicing his saxophone right through the wall. We went over, and he let me try a few notes. Philip said when I come back we'll go hear him play at his club."

"Did you feel . . ." I searched for the right word. "Crowded?"

He shook his head. "The apartment has a balcony and there's a square across the street with a fountain. People sit beside it and play chess. I even saw some jugglers there."

"I wouldn't want to live in the city," I said carefully. "Would you, Cody?"

He shot me a look. "Shana, I'm talking about one day."

I shrugged it off. Beside me, Mama tensed, then gave the rod a little tug. She said. "I believe I've got something."

"Reel!" We were both watching the line, seeing the end of the rod go down. Her hands moved fast and easy against the pull of the fish. We hadn't brought a net, but Cody waded into the stream.

"It's too cold for that," Mama fussed. The fish jumped, and she jerked the line to set the hook. It jumped again, this time close to the bank. Cody followed the line with one hand, grabbed, and came up holding it through the gill.

"A rainbow!" The fish was silver, long and slim. It was too dark to see the pattern on its side. Mama was beside herself.

"It's a nice one too. What do you know about that?"

"Are you going to let it go?"

"I don't think so. This is my first trout, and I want to see how it tastes."

"You ought to put it back," Cody said nervously.

But Mama wouldn't budge. "I'm having it for breakfast."

"Trout are endangered," Cody argued.

"Nonsense. I see them in the grocery store every week."

"Those are farm-raised. That's different."

Mama shook her head. "I'm not going to change my mind."

Cody shrugged then, and gave up.

She fried the fish in butter. The smell got me up, and she cooked a couple of eggs alongside it and gave me half. The flesh was pink, different from bass or bluegill, and the taste was sweet.

"I could go for more of these," Mama said. "I wonder if they're stocked."

I was surprised she asked. "They stock them down the river at Tom's Creek," I said. "Up here they're trying to grow them naturally."

"How'd you know that?"

I colored. "Cody and I met a ranger, and he told us."

"A ranger! You all never mentioned that. I didn't know you saw anybody down here."

"We hardly do."

Mama watched me. "I wondered if you were lonely. Are you glad you spent the summer here?"

I scraped the last bit of fish off my plate. I thought of my secrets: the phone call, the ranger, the cave. "It *was* lonely, but I learned a lot. There're all kinds of birds and flowers that we don't have back home. The gorge is peaceful, too." I shifted uneasily, knowing my answer was mostly a lie, but she didn't seem to notice.

Mama looked at her hands. She had on her wedding ring, and the two rings she'd gotten from Gram: silver rings brought from Scotland by her grandparents, who had settled in North Carolina. "It was true what you said before: that I didn't ask you before I moved us all. That was a mistake. I was so upset by Charlie's leaving that I didn't think things through."

I held my breath.

"I'm not sorry I moved—it was the best thing for me. But as far as you two, I'm not so sure."

She looked right at me. "I want to stay in Laglade a while longer. But that doesn't mean you and Cody have to. I talked to Mike on Tuesday, and he said he'll move back into the old house if you children want to go home for school. I'd come down on the weekends. . . ."

"We wouldn't be together." My voice faltered.

"Not during the week, no. I'd miss you a lot, but I don't want you suffering just so I can feel good about myself." She looked away. "I meant to talk to you together. I'll tell Cody tonight, same as I told you."

"Do you want us to go?" I was thinking of Philip. Maybe Mama guessed that, 'cause she met my eyes.

"No, I'd rather be with you."

"Couldn't you come home, too?"

"Not yet."

"How come?"

"Too many memories, I guess. And moving gave me the chance to meet people with different lifestyles and ideas. I want to take some courses in the fall, and learn new things. If I get the promotion, we'll be able to save some money, too. Maybe next summer we can take a real vacation—you know we always talked about going to Yellowstone, or the Great Lakes."

"Or Hawaii," I said. Mama smiled, but I went on: "What about Daddy?"

She hesitated. "I'm not sure what he wants."

"Have you talked to him?"

A shadow crossed her face. "I have. We're trying to sort out what's best for everyone."

"We used to have so much fun," I said.

She put the back of her hand against my cheek, but she didn't answer.

That whole day I was shook up. On the one hand, Cody and I could finally go home. On the other, Mama wouldn't be there, and what was home without her or Daddy?

But Cody didn't hesitate. That night, as soon as Mama gave him the choice, he said, "Warrensburg."

He couldn't believe I wavered. "You've been talking about going back for months."

"Not as much as you, Cody. Anyway, that was all of us, not just you and me."

"Think about Laglade, Shana—think about what it's like!"

I nodded, but the course directory with its choices stuck like an itch in the back of my mind. Warrensburg was safe, and the house and the river were home. But since Daddy left, Mama wanted something more. Even I'd begun to think of possibilities. I'd met the ranger, explored the gorge, written a poem. At the same time I ached for what had been, and wanted it back.

Eighteen

The next day Cody took me over the Class Three flume. The ranger didn't like the idea, but the two of us stood our ground, and he gave in. There was another life preserver, lumpy and covered with spiderwebs, in the shed; I brushed it off and tied the strap around my waist. Cody paddled upstream, then dragged the canoe over the rocks to the head of the rapid. All I was supposed to do, he explained, was paddle on my right. The ranger stood on the bank below the drop with a throw rope, in case we had problems.

The thing that got me, by hindsight, was the sound. We approached around a curve lined with hemlock, the ripples in the water showing underlying ledges. Fifty yards ahead of us, a flat line marked the edge of the river, which seemed to disappear. An ominous rumble came from below, low at first, then louder.

"When I say paddle, paddle hard," Cody said. "We'll be cutting right, around a set of rocks, then straight down the middle till we hit the pool at the bottom."

"What if we miss?"

"If we miss the right, we'll spin out and go over backward. Most likely the boat will tip, and we'll end up washing through beside it."

"I don't think I want to wash through," I said. Something about the phrase reminded me of the old wringer washer that used to sit on our front porch. You could mash your fingers in it if you weren't careful.

"It's not that bad—I've done it three times. If you fall out, keep your feet up and in front of you."

"What if I bang my head on a rock?"

"Are you chickening out?" The line across the river grew steadily closer.

"I guess not." My heart was thumping. I could see white spray rising somewhere down the drop, and the noise was almost deafening.

"Get ready! Paddle *now*!"

My hands were shaking. I dipped the paddle in the river, took a stroke, tried to lean into it like Cody had showed me. We shot past a rock, then headed toward another outcropping. I felt fear clutch at my throat. I wanted to paddle, but my hands grabbed the sides of the canoe and held on.

"Shana, *paddle!*" Cody's voice came over the roar of

the water, but I wouldn't let go of the boat. I wanted
to close my eyes.

"Shana!"

Cody was furious. I grabbed the paddle and thrust it
in the water just as we hit the drop. The boat bounced
and flew. Spray hit me in the face. I could feel Cody
maneuvering from the rear. We slid past a boulder and
hit thunk on the pool below the flume. Big waves pushed
us to one side. Cody tilted the boat in the other direction, laying his paddle blade almost flat on the water.
The boat straightened and pushed into an eddy right
below where the ranger stood. He looked at me and
shook his head.

"Big baby," Cody said later.

"I didn't know what it was like. You never told me!"

"What do you mean, I never told you? I said it was
great!"

"Great?" I faced him. The ranger looked from one
of us to the other. "I could have drowned," I said coldly.

"You couldn't either. You had on a life jacket, and
Henry was standing right there with a rescue rope. And
it's shallow just beyond the pool. He could have waded
in and pulled you out."

That just made me madder; but the ranger thought
the whole thing was funny. For the first time ever, he
laughed out loud.

"Be quiet!" I snapped; but he only laughed harder.

What got to me, besides how scary it was, was the way they acted together: like they were friends. The ranger never treated me like that. Furthermore, Cody had called him Henry. Wasn't I the one who'd gone to see him first? Wasn't it me who'd bought him food and washed his dishes? How could he treat Cody better than he treated me?

I went and saw him on my own. He wasn't so uppity then; he whined for me to dig more potatoes and carry in a couple buckets of water. "Why don't you ask Cody?" I said.

"He's too light to work that pump."

"So you teach him canoeing, and I'm supposed to do the work."

The ranger fingered his stubbly chin. "I hadn't thought of it like that."

"And he calls you Henry." I knew it sounded childish, but I didn't care.

"You should too. I meant to tell you that. And if you like, I'll give you a few paddling lessons."

I was too disgusted to answer. I thumped myself down and looked at his books. They showed the trout catches from stream to stream in Pennsylvania. I looked up the Leanna, but the tables were confusing.

"These figures represent fly fishing areas, and the others are where the river's stocked," the ranger explained. "But the numbers aren't accurate, because lots of fishermen don't report catches till the season ends September first—that's next week."

I wished I'd had my hands over my ears. He must have seen that on my face. "I guess you'll be starting school," he said.

I nodded. "Cody's going back to Warrensburg."

"And you?"

"I don't know yet. I haven't made up my mind."

"You didn't seem to like that town house."

"I don't. But Mama's staying, and the schools in Laglade are better, too. My English teacher got me started keeping a journal. And the high school has lots of stuff they don't back home."

"Like what?"

"Languages, writing courses . . ." My voice faded.

"You said you wrote a poem."

"I thought you were asleep."

"I'm a light sleeper." The ranger shut the book. "I wouldn't mind hearing it."

I turned red. I'd been carrying the poem folded up in my back pocket, but I was scared to read it out loud. "It isn't any good."

"How do you know?"

A lump came in my throat.

"Read it," he said.

I stumbled through the poem, but when he asked me to do it again, I read it better. Afterward the old man stared at me. "That poem's about me," he said.

"It isn't either. I wasn't thinking of you one bit when I wrote it."

He grunted like he didn't believe me.

"I ought to know who I was thinking of," I said.

He turned cold then. "You're better at poems than canoeing."

"I'm sorry I read it to you."

"I'm not. I liked it."

"You can pump your own water, Henry," I said coldly. I went out and shut the door behind me.

On the way home I took the crumpled paper out of my pocket. I read the poem as if it were something I was proud of:

> *In the grove of the laurels,*
> *In the sound of the rushing stream,*
> *In the patterns of the rainbow trout*
>   *I will seek my name;*
>
> *In the tongues of the river,*
> *In the camps of the Algonquin,*
> *On the green tips of the hemlock branches*
>   *I will seek my name.*

"But you know your name," I told myself. "It's Shana Allen."

The paper stared up at me like an unblinking eye.

Nineteen

————

I got a letter from Daddy. Mama brought it to me a few nights later, while I was still trying to make up my mind about where to live. I took it down to the cave and tore it open.

Darling Shana,

Thank you so much for the beautiful poem. It reminded me of the river and forest that I don't get to see here in New York, and made me homesick.

I think I know what you mean when you say you're seeking your name. Though I named you for someone I admired, everyone has to find their own name. I feel like, at my late age, I'm doing that too!

I've been taking an art course at night, and I still enjoy

*the museum, but I miss you and Cody and Dot more than
ever. I plan to complete my studies and come home by Christmas.*

*Paula Preston, the art student from the Peter Pan, visited
me on her way to Italy—she finally saved up enough for a
one-way ticket! Once I get home, I'm determined to start
saving for the four of us.*

*Love and kisses,
Daddy*

I read the letter twice. I felt limp, worn-out. I wondered if Mama'd got a letter, too, and when I went back
to the cabin I asked her. She shook her head. "Daddy
says he'll be home by Christmas," I told her.

She didn't answer.

"Families are stronger than people on their own," I
said. "Remember how Granddaddy used to drive in four
stakes when he planted a tree? If the wind blew one
stake down, the others would hold."

"I remember," Mama said.

After that my veins felt electric. Daddy was coming
home. All Mama had to do was forgive him. She'd forgiven Granddaddy, or at least tried; and Daddy was her
husband. But thinking about that, I was uneasy. Something had grown in Mama since we moved; each thing
she did without Daddy—patching the roof, taking the

accounting test, even catching the trout—seemed to raise her chin a little higher. Before this summer I'd never heard her talk about poetry, or going to college; and her friends from work seemed to encourage her to try new things. Would she be ready to come home by Christmas? I asked Cody, but he was mad at Daddy and didn't pay that much attention.

"What makes him think he can come back as if he'd never left?" he asked.

"Don't you want him to?"

"Of course. Only . . ."

"Only what?"

"It doesn't even sound like he's sorry."

"I bet he is. He just didn't put it in the letter."

"Furthermore, he should have written to all of us." Cody's fists were clenched. I tried to tickle him but he yanked himself away.

"We'll work it out," I said.

Cody glared as if it was my fault too.

And he was upset about the ranger. "You shouldn't have left him without water, no matter how mad you were," he said. "That was wrong."

"I'll bring some in today."

He nodded. "We got a little, but the pump's hard to work."

That brought up something that was bothering me.

"Cody, how's he going to get along once we're gone?"

"I don't know. I've been thinking about that too." He frowned. "He was okay before we came."

"If what he's got comes and goes, like arthritis, then he might get better. As it is, he can't get to his car to buy food. And he doesn't have a phone. If he did, he could call for help."

Cody rested his chin between his fists. "I don't think it's arthritis. For one thing, his weakness is on one side—his left. That's where he stumbles, and he tapes his left hand to the paddle, too. Remember back in June, when you said his face seemed crooked?"

I nodded.

"I think he'd had a stroke. I looked in a book in the library, and that's a symptom. Since then he's gotten weaker. For all we know, he could have had another one."

"He won't go to a doctor. When I brought it up, he had a fit."

"He has fits over lots of things, but that doesn't mean he can't change. Look how he screamed at us that first time."

"That's true."

"We could ask Mrs. Burns to help him."

I made a face. "She's pretty old herself."

"There isn't anyone else," Cody said.

• • •

That night Mama brought up leaving the cabin.

"I talked to Mike on the phone, and he's going to come up and get Cody and his things," she said. "And you, Shana, if that's what you want."

"When?"

"Not this Sunday, but the following one. School starts Wednesday in Warrensburg, so that'll give you a few days to settle in."

"What about my stuff in Laglade?"

"I can bring it up in my car."

He nodded, like it was all so easy.

Mama looked at me. "Have you figured out what you're going to do?"

"Not yet."

"You need to make up your mind, honey."

"I know." But I kept hoping, if I held out long enough, that I wouldn't have to decide.

Now that Mama'd mentioned leaving, each day along the river was more special. Hidden flowers blooming in a cup of dirt behind a ledge; a row of tiny orange mushrooms; a hummingbird; the murmur of the water by the cave; the first flock of geese, headed south; even the cold air that waked me in the mornings and made me snuggle deeper into my quilt—all fragments of a summer that wouldn't come again. I took long walks and fished the shallow pools, and the deep ones, too. The water had turned colder, so if you snagged your line you cut it instead of wading in to get it back. I caught some suckers and a couple smallmouth, but nothing to brag about.

Cody came back from the ranger's with strange news. "He keeps talking about the canyon. He wants me to paddle him down there and walk back by myself."

"What did you say?"

"No way." He raked the evergreen needles into a pattern with his shoe. "I talked to him about our leaving and said we'd ask Mrs. Burns to help him, but he started yelling, 'I don't want help! All I want is to go through the canyon!' " He looked up at me. "What are we going to do about him, Sha?"

"We'll talk to her anyway. And if she won't help, we'll tell Mama."

Cody reddened. "Tell her we lied all summer?"

"I don't know. I don't know what to do."

I went to see the ranger myself, hoping I could talk some sense into him. He gave me a short paddling lesson and showed me how he checked the fingerlings. He had lists of water temperatures and sediments, which show how muddy the river is. "The cloudier the water, the harder it is for trout to naturalize. They need clear, cold water." He wrote something down. "Every time land gets cleared near a river, especially if it's farmed, that's a death knell for the trout. The rain washes dirt and fertilizer down into the water. To them, that's poison."

"I thought the river was protected."

"It's supposed to be. But I can't be everywhere, and the rules are easy to break. People think if they own the land, they can do whatever they want."

"The Indians knew better than that."

"I'll say they did." He grunted angrily. I tried to help him up, but he brushed me off. Afterward he seemed exhausted. "There's something I want to show you," he said. "You and Cody together."

"What?"

"It's a surprise. Come tomorrow and I'll take you there."

"Is it near the canyon?"

"*No!*" He was so snappish, I didn't have the nerve to ask about Mrs. Burns. I figured Cody and I would do it together, the next day.

Cody was nervous about the surprise. "He asked me to practice more Class Threes. Do you suppose he'll try to trick us into taking him down there?"

"I thought the canyon was Class Four."

"Three, four, and one five: the falls. A guy died there last year. His helmet strap broke on an undercut rock, and his head got bashed in."

"That's horrible."

"You can portage the falls, if you get out soon enough. Even the ranger does."

"How do you know?"

"He's described the rapids. I even know how the river curves, and which way you have to lean."

I groaned. "He has a way of getting what he wants," I said.

We went to his cabin the next day. He was sitting on the bench on the front porch, sound asleep. I was afraid to wake him, but Cody took his arm and gave it a good shake. "We're here, Henry." He startled, stared, shook his head. "It's Cody and Shana."

"You . . ." he mumbled, but he knew who we were. "We'll have to take the boat."

Cody and I looked at each other. "Which way?"

"Upstream," he said. That's why we agreed to go.

They stuck me in the middle, between the thwarts. I wondered how hard it would be, pulling against the current with three of us in the boat; but the ranger started out strong, and Cody's strokes were deep and long. We traveled near the banks and through the eddies, where the current was weaker. I'd never been farther than the flume beyond the ranger's cabin; now Cody and I portaged that, the thwarts digging into our shoulders. The ranger carried the paddles, leaning on them like crutches as he stumbled over the rocky ground. Once around the drop, we launched the canoe from a weedy bank. Wild asters and orange touch-me-nots trailed down to the water. We snaked our way upstream, passing forested banks of hemlock and laurel. Chickadees and titmice twittered in the trees, and a kingfisher flew ahead of us over the water, warning others of our coming with his harsh cry.

"To the right," the ranger murmured. Cody changed his stroke. We sidled along a steep bank laced with roots. "Here," the old man said. But he slipped getting out of the boat, wetting both feet, and that made him mad. He acted like it was our fault. "Both of you can go to hell," he muttered.

"What do you want to show us?"

"I changed my mind." He went and stood by himself. But later he headed upstream, through the thickets. A creek divided the shelf of land that ran along the river, and a rock ridge rose almost perpendicular behind it. He went back there, with us following from a distance. We saw him scrabbling against the wall, pulling back vines. He rubbed his hand across the stone, feeling for something. "You have to promise not to tell," he said. He looked right at us.

"Okay."

"Give me your hand." He took Cody's first, and put it on the rock. Cody traced something with his fingers.

"It's a fish," he told me. "Feel."

I came closer. The picture was outlined on the dark surface of the wall. It reminded me of the Indian ax, and I said so. The ranger nodded. "It's Algonquin," he said. "It's the sign for good fishing. They left it for whoever came along."

I remembered the cup Granddaddy hung beside our spring, so travelers would know the water was safe. But the old man wasn't finished. "Follow me."

He led us up the creek. Abruptly it disappeared among boulders fronting the cliff. We squeezed through a gap between them and stood on a ledge above a pool six feet across. The rock bowl that held it was smooth as silk, and almost white; and the water was pale green.

"A limestone spring." The ranger spoke so softly, his words sounded like prayer. He pushed back through the boulders, but Cody and I stayed. I dipped one hand in the ice-cold water.

"Where does it come from?"

"Somewhere under the ridge," Cody said.

Above us a gust of wind tumbled leaves down the cliff. A bunch cascaded into the spring, rimming the green water with yellow. "We'd better follow him," Cody said.

He was standing arms akimbo on the point where the creek and the river came together. His expression was hard, but I knew by then how frail he really was: so weak that if you bumped him the wrong way, he would fall. I remembered what he'd said before: *I'm holding on. . . .* I thought of the fall leaves with their brittle stems, clinging to the darkening branches. The ranger stared out over the river.

"That spot is sacred," he said. "The Algonquin worshipped it, because its waters multiplied their crops, and grew big fish. The limestone does it. Best fishing in the whole river, right below this creek. . . ."

"The limestone?"

"It neutralizes acids in the water and soil." His eyes were veiled, as if his mind had wandered to another time. "I caught a nineteen-incher on a midge fly right down there. . . ." He pointed to a pool beside a stand of birches. "Don't know what year it was, but I had a fly rod. I wondered if I'd ever bring him in, but I took my time and let him run himself out. I cooked him over hickory chips. . . ." He wet his lips, kept looking down the river. I wasn't sure he remembered Cody and I were there.

"Their wildness settles in you, when you eat them," he said. "They put the river in your bones."

"How do you catch them?" Cody asked.

I thought he'd be mad, but he wasn't. "Worms, minnows—whatever's here naturally. In springtime they like grubs and maggots."

"I thought no one could fish here," I said uneasily. "I thought the government forbid it."

"I'm giving you permission," he said. "Not over and over, but once or twice a year."

I stood there with my mouth hanging open, but Cody said, "Thank you."

I paddled back, with the ranger in the middle. He gave me my second lesson, and by his standards I didn't do well. He fussed at me until he got tired and shut up. When we got to the flume, the ranger and I got out so Cody could run it on his own. He went right through without faltering. When he hit the pool at the base of the drop, the boat landed light and steady as a dancer.

"He's good," the old man said. "One day he'll run the canyon."

"Why'd you ask him to take you there?"

But the ranger wouldn't answer.

Twenty

I think now that the ranger wanted to show us magic. He wanted us hooked on the Leanna, so that wherever we were—in Laglade or Warrensburg, in the house watching TV, reading a book, sitting in the classroom listening to a teacher teaching or droning on and on— our minds, our hearts would be whispering: *River.* He wanted to make sure we'd be back—not just once, but over and over, because the ones who come back are the ones who'll make sure it's treated right: guarded and watched over as zealously as the fingerlings; as carefully and lovingly as the mother cat tends her kittens or the human mother her newborn child.

But he made mistakes. He didn't realize—couldn't, maybe—that we had other loves pulling us too: home and Mama and Daddy and learning new things like writing and paddling a canoe. And he lied: not just once, but lots of times. Maybe you could say he was living a lie. We lied too, about what we'd done all summer, but later we set the record straight, because we had to. There was no one who could force him to come clean.

"He says if I don't take him, he'll go alone," Cody said. We were on our way to Mrs. Burns's house, to talk about the ranger. "He's dead set on going through the rapids one more time."

"That's crazy—he'll never make it."

"He blew up when I said that. He said stay out of his business once and for all."

"He'll change that tune quick enough," I said. "Wait till his food starts running low."

"I guess . . ." Cody looked worried. "Do you think Mrs. Burns will help?"

"We'll have to ask, and see if she says yes. Then we have to get him to accept the help."

"He took ours. . . ."

"I kept going back," I reminded Cody. "And he was still mean about it."

Mrs. Burns seemed glad to see us, and I realized she was probably lonely too, living by herself at the end of that rutted dirt road. She made us chocolate milk. I tried not to look at the telephone while we were waiting. Had

Paula stayed with Daddy as a friend before she left to catch her plane? Or was there more to it? Did he love her, even for a little while? I trembled, sitting there, but Mrs. Burns came back in and Cody gave me a look that meant begin.

"There's a ranger living a few miles up the river in a cabin with no phone or running water," I said slowly. "He works for the federal government, raising trout. Over the summer he's been sick. Now he's too weak to get to his car, or pump his own water."

Mrs. Burns nodded, and I thought she wanted me to go on, but instead she said, "Maybe I should have warned you about Henry. But he hasn't been bothering people like he used to, so I hoped he'd stay away."

Cody and I stared.

"He's not a ranger," she explained. "That's a story he made up. His uniforms come from the fish hatchery where he used to work. They fired him because he couldn't get along with anyone. Things had to be done his way or not at all."

She shook her head. "The sheriff threatened to arrest him three years ago for harassing fishermen. After that he swore he'd stop. He pretends he's in charge of the river, but he only owns that little cabin and the land it sits on." Mrs. Burns sighed. "I knew his wife," she said. "She was a nice girl, and she cared about him too. But she got lonely down there by herself. She couldn't even watch TV."

"Are you sure he's not a ranger?" Cody asked. Then Mrs. Burns realized we'd been duped.

"I should have warned you," she said.

"But he *is* sick," Cody said. I had to admire him for not giving up.

"I'll call the sheriff—they'll bring him out," Mrs. Burns said. "They tried to put him in a nursing home last year. They think he's getting senile. I laughed when the sheriff told me that. 'You don't know Henry,' I said. 'He's been nuts for forty years. Not just crazy—mean, too.' "

Cody and I just sat there.

"You're not the first to try to help him," she added. "A social worker went there in April, and he threatened her with a gun."

I stood up. "You don't need to call," I said. "Thanks, anyway."

"He didn't threaten you, did he?"

"No, ma'am."

"Have you had a good summer?"

I had to answer, 'cause Cody had his hand on the doorknob and I could tell he wasn't looking back.

"Very good," I said. "Thanks again."

Mama had news for me the next morning before she left for work. "I saw an old man in a canoe when I got up. He was heading down the river a mile a minute."

Soon as she started up the ridge, I woke Cody and

told him. He whipped the quilt off and grabbed his pants. "He's going for the canyon."

"I thought he wanted you to take him."

"He knows I won't."

"That's crazy. Weak as he is, he'll never make it through."

"I know." Cody was tying his sneakers. He stuck a knife and some string in his jeans pocket. "I'm going after him."

I stood there for a minute, not sure what to do or say. "He lied to us, Cody. Most of what he said was lies."

"Once I stop him, I'll tell him we found out."

"I'm coming too."

We grabbed a couple oranges and a hunk of cheese and took off down the river.

The first part was easy. We knew where the trails went and, after they stopped, how to scramble over the rocks without hitting a dead end. We went a couple of miles that way, though it was slow going staying on one side of the river. Chilly as it was, we didn't want to cross unless we had to.

There were no signs of him, though I don't know what we were looking for. We hustled between thickets. Briars tore at my shirt, and my socks were covered with hitchhikers. Once I had to stop and rest. "Why don't we say to hell with him?" I asked Cody.

"Would you?"

I faltered then. "I don't know."

"We wouldn't know what happened, or why he went," Cody said. "And he did teach us things. He showed us the Indian picture, and the spring."

"Why did he lie?"

"Shana—look!" Cody pointed. The tail of a red fox disappeared around a fallen tree not forty feet away.

"There might be kits!"

"We don't have time to look," Cody said.

After a while the south side of the river got too dense for bushwhacking. Cody thought the north looked better, and I did too. We found a shallows, took off our shoes and socks, rolled our pants, and waded over. The cold water was a shock, but at least we had dry socks when we got to the other side. "Hypothermia," Cody muttered as we put them on.

"What's that?"

"Exposure to cold air or water drops your body temperature. If it stays low, you die."

"I'm not *that* cold."

"I'm not talking about you."

The thought of the ranger in the water moved us faster. We pushed through high weeds until the old rail line swooped down from the north for us to follow. That made walking easier, though trees between the water and the track hid parts of the riverbed. Every few minutes we climbed down the bank onto some rocks and looked around. But there was only the river, quiet in some stretches, other places rushing and foaming like a rabid animal. My legs felt like sticks about to break. "What if he's already in the canyon?" I asked.

"We'll have tried to stop him." Cody peeled the skin back from a piece of orange, swallowed it down.

"What if he's . . ." My voice dried up before I finished the question.

"Come on," Cody said.

This time we kept our shoes on and waded downstream on the left, where the riverbed was shallow. It only took us a few minutes to find him. He must have crawled out of the river, 'cause he was lying on a gravel bar with his feet still in the water and his head covered with blood. There were flies buzzing around like he was dead, and for a moment I thought he was. Then I pulled off his life preserver and saw his chest moving. I put my fingers on the inside of his wrist while Cody hauled his feet out of the water. His skin felt clammy, and the pulse was so fast and weak, I thought it might stop any second. I didn't want to look at his head, but after a bit I turned it toward me. His eyes were shut, and the left side of his face was thick with blood. A deep wound from temple to eyebrow was still bleeding. I took my bandanna out of my pocket and pressed it there. Within a half minute it was soaked.

"He hit his head on a rock," Cody muttered. "He must have lost control of the canoe—maybe there." He pointed. "The boat flipped, but he managed to make it to shore."

"He's lost a lot of blood."

Cody was pale himself. Suddenly he turned and retched. I remembered, when we were little, how he used to cover his head with a blanket if someone got shot on TV. I felt my stomach rising too, but I closed my eyes and willed it down.

We sat there for a moment. I couldn't help thinking how ridiculous that was, the two of us sitting while his head was pumping blood like a piston. But it was pointless to call for help: There was no one to hear us. Cody must have been thinking the same thing.

"There's cabins at the junction with Tom's Creek," he said. "I saw them on the map."

"There's no way to walk around the canyon." We both knew that. My heart was hammering against my ribs.

Cody said, "He told me I was good."

"We can't trust anything he said."

"Shana . . ." Cody was calm now, as if he'd thought things through. "It's three hours back to the cabin, and then we'd have to walk to Mrs. Burns's. The route downstream is a half hour at the most. There're phone lines and a paved road. I'd be talking to a doctor in forty minutes."

"They can't get here anyway."

"They can send a helicopter—they'll lower a stretcher and a medic, like they do on television."

"You'd never make it alone." I stared at Cody. "I'm older, and I'm telling you: You can't go."

He wouldn't look at me. "I won't sit here and watch him die."

"You're not going down that river by yourself."

"Shana—" He was practically begging.

That was when I figured it out. Maybe I was afraid to see someone die, or maybe I was trying to protect Cody, though if you think it through, there was no sense to that. "I'm going with you," I said.

"You?"

I nodded. I read the thoughts that crossed his mind, knew he wouldn't speak them because if he did we wouldn't go. Finally he said, "This time you'll have to paddle."

"I will."

"If you paddle, we might make it." His voice was thoughtful, considering.

"I'm not afraid." My voice quavered.

He looked at me and shook his head. "I'll go find the canoe," he said. "It's probably swamped somewhere downstream." He took off down the river.

I sat beside the ranger while I waited for Cody. I kept the bandanna pressed against his cut. Now and then I rinsed it, wrung it out, and put it back. After a little while the bleeding slowed, but his heartbeat raced, and it seemed to me his breathing grew faster and more shallow. I tried to tell him everything would be all right, but he didn't seem to hear. Then I remembered that he'd lied to us, and how mad and hurt we'd been. That's when I decided to tell the truth.

"You may die," I said, forcing the words out one by one. "You've lost a lot of blood, and who knows whether we'll make it down the river to get help." Flies buzzed around his eyes, and I swished them away.

"I want you to know that Cody and I found out you aren't a ranger after all. You tricked us and made it stick for the whole summer. You didn't need to do that. We would have listened to what you had to say whether you were a ranger or not. We would have been *interested*. Instead, we don't know what to believe, except one thing, and that is, you're a fake."

Horribly, like a ghost in a dead man's skin, the ranger stirred. I'd thought he couldn't hear me, but I went on:

"You put us in danger," I said. "You knew if you came down here Cody'd follow you. He's looking for your boat. When he comes back, we're going through the canyon to get help. You said not to count on people, and that's fair, I guess; but if I get through and Cody dies, I'll blame you forever."

A breeze stirred up and down the river, soft as baby's breath. I was glad no one would know how I'd treated the ranger when he was hurt. I thought of my granddaddy then: lying in a strange bed, sick with cancer, away from the people and places that he loved.

That softened me, I guess, or maybe I just felt I'd had my say. I took his pulse again and touched his hand. It was only faintly warm. Down the river a buzzard drifted in slow circles, so high his wings were smaller than a postage stamp. I'd seen them before, circling like that: waiting for some suffering squirrel or muskrat to give up the ghost. The ranger gasped, then kept breathing. Beside him the Leanna droned and murmured. I wiped away the blood and put my mouth close to his ear.

"What you did to us was wrong, and you shouldn't have put Felix in that cage, either," I said. "But you did it for the river. And it's here, with you. If you listen, you can hear it."

He nodded. I started crying then. I thought of Granddaddy and Daddy, and now Henry.

"People leave," I mumbled. "I hate that."

I watched to see if he would nod again, but he didn't.

Twenty-one

Cody came around the bend, pulling the canoe. He'd had to go almost to the mouth of the canyon to get it back. The good thing was, there was another life jacket in the ranger's gear bag, and a helmet, too. We knew he kept an extra paddle duct-taped to the inside of the boat. Cody fumbled with the helmet straps, muttering, "Why didn't he wear it?"

" 'Cause he's a stubborn old fool." I was crying. I put on the life jacket, cinched it tight. We argued about the helmet, but Cody said since I'd be in the bow, I should wear it. My hands were shaking so bad, he had to fasten it. He pulled the canoe out from the bank and looked at me. "Are you sure you want to go?"

I nodded. He patted the ranger's shoulder, got into the boat. I bent over the old man.

"I'll be back," I whispered. "Wait for me."

I climbed into the canoe and pushed off. I only looked back once. I could see his legs and brown rubber boots sticking out from behind the curve of the gravel bar. I felt queasy, like I might faint, but Cody stared at me hard. "You can't panic like you did before."

"I won't!"

"Then paddle hard."

I knelt and dug the blade in deep, pushed the water back like I was shoveling earth in a garden. To my surprise the boat leaped forward.

"That's where it starts." Cody nodded toward a spot ahead of us where the ridges rose high and the river narrowed. There was a little space to pass through, like a door. My heart began to slam against my ribs. A muffled booming came from the canyon, like the engine of Uncle Mike's old truck. "Get ready—*now*!"

I pushed with all my strength. We passed through the door, into white water. We caught the downside of a wave and the boat took off like it had wings.

"*Right!*" Cody shouted. I paddled hard. The noise was deafening. Pale tongues of water lapped the sides of the canoe, and a boulder slipped by, then another, both of them close enough to touch. The current twisted left, and we went with it, down a narrow chute into calmer water.

"We did it!"

Since Cody was behind me, I couldn't see his face, but he sounded cautious. "Four more to go, Shana . . ."

"Four more!" I echoed, but I couldn't help feeling proud. I wished the ranger could have seen me paddle! I sat back on the seat for just a minute. My knees were wet and clammy. Water sloshed back and forth in the bottom of the canoe, but there was nothing to bail with. Cody used his paddle blade to splash some of it over the side.

"Dog's Breath's next," he said. "There'll be standing waves as we approach it, but if we head straight into them, they won't upset us."

I looked ahead. The high walls of the canyon shaded the river most of the way across, but I could see moving hills of water—the standing waves, I guessed—and, beyond them, an outcropping of rocks.

"Which way do we go?"

"Right. Look for an eddy above those boulders where we can pull up and look the rapid over. The ranger said there's a clear diagonal path across the current, but I'd like to see it before we get started, so we can plan our route."

"What if we miss the eddy, or there isn't one?" I looked back.

He shrugged his thin shoulders. "We'll have to do the best we can."

I got back on my knees. We started paddling hard just before we hit the standing waves, and though they looked big, we cut through them without a hitch. The noise was picking up, so that it was hard to talk. The rapid approached fast, as if it were rushing toward us. I tried to guess where Cody wanted us to pull over. "To the *right!*" he yelled, and I saw a pool there, but the current was pushing us the other way. I stabbed my paddle in and swung wide; the bow hit the eddy, but Cody's end was sliding away. *"Dig!"* he screamed, and I dug like some cartoon creature, like Woody Woodpecker or the cat in *Tom and Jerry*, paddling so fast and hard my arms seemed like a windmill. Ever so slowly the canoe slipped into the pool. Below us, boulders big as the cab of Daddy's truck stood shoulder to shoulder, water crashing off them in sheets. "I'm so scared," I said; but Cody couldn't hear. He shrieked over the noise: "Remember what I said?"

My mind went blank. *"What?"*

"We're paddling on a diagonal—there to there." He showed me with one arm. "You paddle on the left unless I tell you to switch." He paused, took a deep breath. "When I say go!"

I closed my eyes for just a second.

"Ready, set, go!"

I opened them and dug the paddle in. We shot like an arrow across the current. Below us the rocks stood like a wall, but I kept paddling, and just as I thought we'd be swept upon them, Cody turned the boat and we slid by. A wave caught the bow and soaked me.

"Two down!" Cody yelled.

I couldn't stop shaking. After a minute he noticed. "You cold, Sha?"

Not just cold, I thought; but I nodded.

"We've got another half mile before Deerfoot. If we move over, we can paddle in the sun."

To our left a narrow band of sunlight played among the waves. The river had calmed now, and was rocking us gently. My heart stopped pounding, and I had time to look around: Scraggly trees sprouted from the sides of the canyon, and the dark shapes of deer moved along the crest of a high ridge. The sun felt good on my back and shoulders.

Cody began to review what lay ahead. "Deerfoot's a Class Four, but the ranger said for a four it's not too bad. Then comes Blindman's Falls—there's a portage going off to the right just before it, so we'll beach the boat and carry it around. The last rapid's an easy Class Three. The cottages are a half mile beyond that."

"What's Deerfoot like?" I tried to keep my voice steady.

"Two oblong chutes go around a rock island—they say from above it looks like a cleft hoof. The hard part's that the current piles into the rock. You can either hug the wall on the far right or else cross to the eddy just above the island and then shoot off to the left."

"What do you want to do?"

"Hug the right wall." Cody had to shout, because the canyon was starting to echo the roar of white water. Up ahead spray hung like mist over the Leanna. "Remember the pry stroke?"

I showed him, sliding the paddle perpendicular, to the left side of the boat and pushing away. The canoe slid to the right.

"You'll have to do it harder than that."

"You sound like Henry," I muttered, but of course Cody didn't hear.

We pulled closer to the rapid. Deerfoot didn't seem worse than the others, but the river had a dark, boiling look, like the surface of a witch's cauldron. I noticed that the swirling currents made it hard for the paddle to grab hold. We stayed to the far right, but like before, the current tried to push us toward the middle. Twenty feet before the island Cody started yelling: "Pry!" I pushed the paddle with all my strength, but it didn't make any difference. *"Pry!"* he screamed again, but terror gripped me, and I couldn't move. We were sliding away from the right wall. Then he must have given up, 'cause I heard his voice faintly through the roar of the rapid: "Center eddy, Shana—*paddle hard!*"

"Left or right?" I wondered vaguely. The water

crashed around me. I chose left and started pushing. The island was coming at us like a bus in the wrong lane of a highway. Before, Cody had turned us at the last minute. I took a deep breath and paddled like crazy. Then we were grabbed by a huge wave. I hoped we'd slide off into the eddy, but instead it dropped us smack into the center of the island. *"Hold on to your paddle!"* Cody screamed. We hit the rock with a horrible grinding sound. The boat flipped to the right. We hung in midair for a split second; then the river rose to meet us and the canoe heaved onto its side like a dying whale. I was pulled under by the current, tumbled upside down, back up, all under the crushing weight of water. It was cold and dark, and I was running out of air. I pushed for the surface, pushed again. Pictures tumbled through my mind: a bird, a book, the ranger's brown boots. I kicked again; then I was gulping air, but the bottom dropped from under and I was flung like a fish into brightness. Looking down, I saw that I was going over a drop. I hit the pool with a splash, went under, came back up. I stuck my feet up, like Cody had told me to. *Cody!* Where was Cody? Then I saw him, clinging to a rock near the right bank. I was flooded with relief.

"Cody, I'm here! I'm all right! Cody!"

He looked up. His face was white. He said something I couldn't hear.

"I'm keeping my feet up, like you said!" I shouted.

He gestured toward the right bank, spoke again.

I tried to paddle toward him, but I couldn't. Drifting past, I finally heard what he was shouting: *"Get out, Shana! The falls! The falls!"*

If you've ever lived a nightmare, you know it doesn't end when the action's over. It hovers in the back of your mind, emerging when you least expect it; so that coming upon some ordinary place you're suddenly frightened, and you have to summon courage to go on. Recalling Cody's shout, I tremble even now. The water spun me like a twig; the right bank was close, but beyond my reach. "Keep trying, Shana!" I heard from behind, and I pushed and kicked. Then the paddle, clasped in my right hand, scraped something, and I shoved it down and felt the riverbed. I pushed off the bottom toward the right, then again. Cody was up now, splashing along the edge, his arm toward me: "The paddle! Here!" I managed to hoist it toward him. He grabbed the blade and pulled: "Hold on!" My legs touched rock. He dragged me to a shallows, hovering beside me as if he still thought I might get swept away. I was shaking all over.

"You okay, Sha?"

I couldn't say yes, not then; but after a minute I said, "Thanks."

Cody nodded. "Can you stand up?"

I tried. To my surprise, my legs held me.

"The ranger," Cody murmured. We could see the

swamped canoe above the portage, twenty feet down-stream. "Come on," Cody said. "Let's go."

It turned out Cody'd wrenched his wrist in the river, so I did most of the work, snagging the boat, emptying it, dragging it over the path. I could hear Blindman's Falls roaring on my left. Cody looked at it, but I didn't want to. Later he told me it was bad.

This time I sat in the stern, since Cody could hardly paddle. For some reason that didn't throw me. We shoved off, with the rapid crashing behind us.

"Only one more," Cody said. The walls of the canyon started to recede. I must have got a second wind, because my paddling was shooting us forward. Cody noticed too.

"Henry wouldn't believe it was you," he said.

The last rapid came then: a set of boulders with a chute right down the middle. Cody ruddered from his side, grasping the paddle by the blade with his good hand. I paddled hard, and we swooped over the drop and right on through. A great blue heron, fishing behind a rock, turned and rose on wings that stretched taller than me. Somewhere in the distance a car ground over pavement. After a while we saw three houses clustered on the bank like comfortable old friends.

"I'm going to write this down," I told Cody. "The whole summer, but starting with today."

"No one will believe you." He pointed suddenly. "Look—phone lines. And there's a man, chopping wood."

We pulled up the canoe and went toward him. My legs were shaking so bad. I could hardly walk.

"Someone's hurt up the river. We'd like to use the phone to call for help."

He held out his hand. "Come inside."

He called the shock/trauma unit at the hospital in Harrisburg. They said the helicopter would pick me up so I could show them where the ranger was. The stranger promised Cody a ride home.

The helicopter trip was noisy and fast, with me sitting up front beside the pilot. He gawked over the canyon, asking how we'd made it through, but I was so nervous about Henry I could hardly speak. He looked tiny and still on the gravel bar, and I thought for sure that he was dead. They lowered me down in a harness, with a medic and a stretcher right behind.

"He's alive," she shouted over the din of the helicopter. "What's his name?"

"Henry Luck."

"Did you see it happen?"

I shook my head.

"How do you know him?"

"He lives up the river."

She'd taken his pulse by then and given him a shot. She taped the head wound quickly. "He's lost a lot of blood. Tell his family to come fast. . . ." She hesitated, then looked around nervously as if she'd never seen a wild place before. "Can you get home?"

"Yes."

She strapped him down. "Is he a friend?"

I don't know why, but I nodded.

"He's lost a lot of blood," she repeated. She looked at me to see if I understood. I held his hand for a second. "We made it through the canyon," I said. I tried to let go, but he clung on. I knew then he was scared.

"Henry," I said, "good-bye."

He was holding on, clinging on. The medic moved impatiently. "We've got to go."

"Henry . . ."

He gripped my hand like it could save him. His mouth moved, but nothing came out. Suddenly I knew what he wanted. For a second I was angry. "I can't do it," I said.

The medic looked confused.

"I'm going back to school," I tried to explain. "I won't be here, except maybe a few weekends."

Henry held on. I remembered saying to Cody he has a way of getting what he wants. I shook my head, but he looked so frightened. I couldn't stand for him to leave like that.

"I'll try to take care of it," I said.

That was when he let me go.

Twenty-two

We found out the ranger died. The medic told Mama he didn't even make it to the hospital. He died in the helicopter, with all that noise. I wonder if he opened his eyes and looked out at the patchwork of rocks, trees, and river. Maybe he saw what the wild geese see when they swoop low over the ridges on their way to some-place else.

Cody and I grieved his death. We sat together under the hemlocks and said we'd miss him no matter what Mama thought. I showed Cody a new poem:

I dream of Henry,
   standing fit and strong
   at the edge of a river;

He does not see where the black bear
  laps water
  or the mountain lion, with full belly,
    suckles her cubs in a den on the hemlock ridge;

But songbirds bright with color
  flutter around him,
  and every flower—phlox, violet, touch-me-not—
    has chosen this day to bloom.

The fish are thick in the water
  as he snaps his rod:
  the line rolls back,
  comes forward in a perfect arc;

And the largest trout
  in the clear, deep pool
  prepares to rise.

Cody had his own way of remembering Henry. He claimed he was going to keep paddling till he was good enough to do Class Fours. When he turned eighteen, he'd run big rivers: the Cheat, the Gauley, and the Tygart. "And I'm going to learn the saxophone," he said.

"What's that got to do with rivers?"

"Nothing, except I heard it this summer, and it sounds so cool, Shana—like a waterfall, only it's music."

"Do you think you'll find a teacher back home?"

He shrugged. "I bet Uncle Mike will drive me to Oldtown. I know there'll be somebody there."

I felt like saying, There'd be someone in Laglade. That's where I'd be starting high school. When Mama found out how much I'd lied over the summer, she said she didn't trust me on my own. Cody stood right there and heard her say it, and he didn't stick up for me, either. I guess he was afraid she'd change her mind about him, too. Mama knew what we were thinking—she said I was the one in charge. When I tried to explain what happened, she shook her head and said she didn't even want to know.

The day the bandage came off Cody's wrist, he went out fishing. After he left, someone knocked on the cabin door. I thought it might be Uncle Mike, come early; but when I looked out, two men in uniforms were standing there. The older one, fat and with a mustache, tipped his broad-brimmed hat: "I'm Sheriff Cooper, looking for Mrs. Allen."

I called to Mama, and she went to the door with a face that said *What next?*

The sheriff introduced himself and his deputy. "We been over to Henry Luck's cabin yesterday. We knew he kept a gun, and we didn't want it lying around where somebody could walk in and take it. Turned out there weren't any bullets, but we picked it up and cleared out the food, and burned the trash and dirty clothes." He cleared his throat and looked at Mama kind of funny.

"It's the second time I've been there this month. Some fishermen complained about him, and I went by a couple weeks ago to say he'd better stop that nonsense. Then I saw how bad he looked. I asked him if he didn't want to visit the senior home in town, just to see what it's like. He didn't blow up like he did last time, but he took this paper off his desk and asked me to witness it; and so I did.

"I said I'd come back Tuesday and drive him into town. To my surprise he said okay. Said he had a couple things to take care of first. Next thing you know, I heard that he was dead.

"I found this on his desk." The sheriff held out a piece of paper. "You're Shana Allen, aren't you?"

She pulled back like the words stung. "That's my daughter."

My heart started banging, but he didn't hand the paper to me. He gave it to Mama, and she read out loud:

"To whom it may concern:

I, Henry Luck, being of sound mind, do hereby declare this to be my last will and testament. I bequeath my land, my house, and its contents to Shana Allen and her brother, Cody.

"It's signed and dated last week." Mama stared at the paper. "Is it legal?"

The sheriff cleared his throat. "Reckon so. Hope you don't mind, but I took the liberty of telling his ex-wife and daughter about it, being as they're from around here. It's no contest far as they're concerned."

"Shana's just thirteen."

"I don't think anyone's going to make a fuss over it. The cabin's just one room, and there's no road access to the place; no utilities, either—the stove and refrigerator run on propane. I checked the taxes, and they're eighty dollars, paid up last spring."

"Shana?" Finally Mama spoke to me. "Did you know about this?"

I took the paper in my hands. His old scrawly handwriting reminded me of him: wobbly but stubborn. I wondered when he'd done it. Was that what he was trying to tell me on the riverbank, before they took him away?

I swallowed. "No."

"Why would he leave it to you?" Mama asked.

"He wanted us to care for certain things," I tried to explain. "The river, and the trout. Maybe he thought we needed a place to work from. He didn't approve of this one, 'cause of the outhouse."

"You're children," Mama said. "How could you care for a river?"

I didn't answer. The sheriff smiled.

"He wasn't right in the head, ma'am. But Ada Burns said the youngsters helped him out, and maybe he was thinking of that. He never did anything regular; wasn't that sort of person. He was as ornery as any man I ever met."

I looked at the sheriff, and he smiled, and I saw that he knew Henry. Maybe he even liked him a little. He nodded at me.

"Not many have their own place at your age, young lady. Maybe that's what you get in return for a kindness."

My eyes filled up then, and he looked embarrassed.

"File the paper in the probate court," he told Mama. "They'll stamp it in a month or two; then it's hers. In the meantime I locked it up, but it's awful messy, so here's the key." He handed it to me.

Twenty-three

The only good thing about Cody's leaving was seeing Uncle Mike. He hadn't heard about the ranger, so he wrapped his arms around me and asked, "Coming home, Sha?"

"I can't." He must have seen from my face there was something wrong.

"How come?"

I didn't want to tell, so I went outside while Mama was explaining. When I came back in, he still looked baffled. But he must have decided not to question Mama's judgment, 'cause he hugged me and said, "We'll see you at Thanksgiving, if not before."

We showed him around the river and the woods. He wanted to see the ranger's cabin, but Mama said there wasn't time. She hadn't even gone up there to see it herself, though I'd asked her to. Maybe she couldn't accept that something good had come out of the whole thing.

We ate our lunch together, hamburgers cooked outside on the fire ring Cody and I had built. I remembered how we'd found those salamanders and played with them. Then we realized Uncle Mike hadn't met Felix. Cody ran around looking for him. We'd agreed he'd go to Warrensburg, 'cause Laglade was no place for an outdoor cat.

But Felix didn't come, or wouldn't; he could be perverse, especially if he knew you wanted him to do something. We checked the top shelf in the pantry, a hole in the foundation of the house, the tall hemlock where warblers and jays attacked and tried to drive him down. Cody was getting upset. It seemed like he'd be able to leave us if he had Felix, but he couldn't go without him.

"Damn cat," he said. His voice was half dried up.

"I'll start toting your stuff to the truck," Uncle Mike said. "Maybe if he sees you're really leaving, the rascal will come out."

Mama walked with Mike. I guess she was telling him more about the rotten stuff I'd done, and how I couldn't be trusted. Cody was trying not to cry.

"You went through all those rapids," I told him. "Now you're falling apart over a cat."

He shook his head and looked away.

"We'll bring him down on a weekend," I said.

Cody didn't answer. I got the feeling there were things between us, things besides Felix, that needed to be said.

"I wouldn't have gone home with you, even if I'd had the choice," I told him. "I thought about it a lot, and I want the school in Laglade. They care about what you think, instead of just the right answers. And most of the kids go on to college. They even have an office to help with scholarships."

"Won't you miss being outdoors?"

"I can come up here on weekends, or even after school. And it won't last forever—Mama said she just wanted to stay a while longer."

Cody wouldn't look at me. Maybe he didn't believe me, or maybe he was hurt I wouldn't have gone with him. "You shouldn't have gotten all the blame," he muttered.

"You told me not to go back to the ranger's."

"At first I did. But I went up there myself, when he offered the canoeing."

I shrugged.

"Anyway, Mama's wrong," Cody said suddenly. "And I was too. Because if you hadn't gone, we wouldn't have known him. They can say he's crazy—maybe he was; but he knew what kind of life he wanted, and when to end it. He couldn't have lived in that old folks' home."

I nodded. I felt like throwing my arms around Cody when he said that, but I knew he'd get mad.

"They don't know certain things," Cody said. "Like the fish carved in the cliff, and the limestone spring."

"Keep secrets," I told him; and we hooked our pinky fingers around each other's like we used to when we were small.

Felix came out while we were talking. If there was ever an animal that wanted to know your secrets, it was that cat. We grabbed him fast. He guessed that something was up, and he hissed and spat, but we held on for dear life.

"Next time you come home, bring the canoe," Cody said once he was in the truck.

Mama looked at him and shook her head. I could tell she didn't want him running any more rapids.

"Take good care of our cabin," Cody told me. He was holding Felix up to look out the window.

"Good-bye!"

I felt like running along behind him, grabbing on, but I held myself back and watched as they pulled away.

We stayed five more days on the Leanna. I was counting down: days and family—four, three, two. Mama'd taken vacation that last week, and she kept a tight rein on where I went and what I did. I asked to go to the ranger's, but she always had some reason to say no. Maybe she thought keeping me away would lessen what had happened. But I felt shackled, after the freedom of those months with Cody.

We couldn't get along. She was cold, because of what I'd done, and I was mad she wouldn't listen to my explanations. When I mentioned the ranger, she got this look like he was an ax murderer. After a while I gave up. I missed Cody like crazy. Thinking of him back at the house, sitting on the front porch or walking through the field toward the river, made me shiver with longing and regret.

Twice, at night, I slipped out the bedroom window and went to the cave. I balanced my flashlight on the shelf and wrote in my journal, explaining the things Mama wouldn't listen to. I wrote another poem, and started the story of the summer, a story it would take me years to finish.

I was so lonely I was desperate. One day Mama took me with her to the grocery store. I said I'd stay in the car and read, but the truth was I'd noticed a pay phone in a corner of the parking lot, and as soon as she got inside the store, I dialed the New York operator and told her Daddy's number. This time I was prepared: If a woman answered, I'd ask to speak to him as if she wasn't even there. The phone started ringing, and I rehearsed what I wanted: to have him hear about the ranger, and be sad that he was dead. Daddy could grieve a mouse or even a flower. He used to help us bury dead pigeons, and say prayers over their graves. The phone rang four times. Then a voice said, "The number you have dialed has been disconnected. . . ." I asked the operator to check it for me. She couldn't find another listing for Daddy. I kept asking and asking, and she seemed glad when I gave up.

I didn't tell Mama about the call. What was the point in telling her? 'Cause Mama was unhappy too. At night, when she thought I was asleep, I heard her crying. It was such a lonely sound, in that lonely cabin, and I had to lie there and listen. Sometimes I tried to hold my ears to keep it out. But later the wind blew down the ridge, and the trees moaned, and it seemed as if the whole world was grieving.

Star light, Star bright,
   Take me home. . . .

Lift me like mist over the ridges
   to the farmhouse by the field;
Carry me like foam on dark water
   rushing to the place
         where I was born;

Let me rise from the riverbank
   where honeysuckle fills the air with sweetness
   and crickets sing my name;
And find the light in the back-room window
      softly glowing;
         shining
            for me.

The fourth day I started packing. I got out my duffle bag and threw in shorts and T-shirts, socks and underwear, the holey sneakers I used for fishing, a couple pairs of worn jeans. I got my journal from the cave and the nature guides I kept down there. My tackle box went into the crate I'd had beside the bed, along with the map, knife, flashlight, and some pretty stones I'd found by the water. I put Daddy's letters on top.

I cleaned up the room, too. I swept out the dead leaves and bits of bark from the whittling I'd told Cody to do outside. The broom hit something hard under the bed. I got down on my knees and saw the picture box! Had Cody left it for me? I dragged it out and opened the flaps. He'd looked through it last, because the snapshots on top were his favorites: our family sitting at the table at Thanksgiving, or posed on the running board of Daddy's rig. Here we were by the river, holding stringers of fish we'd caught on a float trip; and by the Christmas tree, with Granddaddy in his nightshirt, a Santa Claus hat on his head. Under that was a picture I'd forgotten: an old woman looking down at an infant, her face wreathed with smiles. The baby peered back with solemn eyes. Those are my eyes, I realized; and that's Gram, holding me. I thought I remembered her voice, reading out loud; and I'd been told how, in the year before she died, when she was too sick to walk, I'd try to climb into her lap. She'd move her quilting first, so I wouldn't get stuck by pins. I traced the squares in the quilt in my bed: mostly dark colors, greens and blues and browns, with a few stripes and patterns. Mama'd said Gram made it from old clothes. A patch covered with purple flowers came from the overalls I'd worn when I first learned to crawl. They were so full of holes, Daddy'd thrown them in the trash; but Gram had made him fish them out again. She'd searched until she found a square that was salvageable. "She made stuff from other people's castoffs," Granddaddy told me once. "Good things: rugs and quilts from rags; feather pillows; apple jelly from the peels I would have thrown away. . . ."

I put the picture box in my crate and wandered into the big room. Mama was sitting at the table reading papers. When I came in she set them aside.

"Are you done packing?"

"Almost."

"I've got most of the pots and dishes put away." She showed me a cardboard box. "We'll have to make lots of trips to the car."

"I'll make one now." I half expected her to say she'd go along; but she didn't, and as I walked back down the trail, I felt a little better. The cabin looked neat and tidy on its perch partway down the ridge: We'd sealed the windows with plastic; the roof was patched and tarred; downed wood was chopped and stacked along one wall. We'd helped the place along, and it had sheltered us. I went into the house. Mama was bent over papers—the ones she'd put aside before, I thought.

"Are those your scores from the accounting test?"

She shook her head, but for the first time in what seemed like days, she smiled. "No, but I passed. In fact, I did well. Philip thinks I'll get the promotion."

"That's good." I tried to sound enthusiastic. Mama picked up on that.

"I know things have been hard between us, Sha, but they'll get better. I was just so shocked by what happened, and how little I knew about what was going on. I've thought about it, and I realize how you got sucked in. You must have thought I'd take you back to Laglade if I found out about the ranger. There's some truth to that. . . ." She nodded as if I'd said it and she was agreeing. "I don't condone what you did, but I blame myself, too. I was so preoccupied making a life for myself that I didn't pay enough attention to you and Cody."

"The ranger was strange, but he was interesting, too," I told Mama.

"Interesting?" She blinked as if we'd gotten off course.

But I persevered. "Cody liked him once he got to know him. He could be childish, but he wanted what was best for the river. And he wanted us to love it, like he did."

"Oh." The look on Mama's face told me she couldn't

imagine loving a river; or maybe she just thought loving people was hard enough. She changed the subject, asking about school clothes and what I thought I'd need. But I wasn't ready to move forward, not yet.

"Over the summer I kept a journal," I told her. "I started a story, and I wrote three poems."

"You'll have to read them to me." Mama was smiling.

I don't know why I said the next thing, it was so stupid; and maybe, if I hadn't, the whole summer would have ended only halfway rotten, though I doubt it. "I read one to the ranger, and I sent it to Daddy, too. He said it reminded him of himself."

Mama's face must have changed, but I didn't notice that yet, because I was rushing blindly ahead, letting my hopes hang out like bright-colored laundry on a clothesline. "When he comes back, we'll sit around the oil stove after supper and read poetry," I said. "We'll have popcorn, and Cody'll pick something dumb like 'Casey at the Bat,' and Daddy can read one from the Renaissance, and you choose one of your favorites, the 'Daffodils,' or something new. I'll read the poems I wrote myself. You all will be the first to hear them."

I stopped suddenly, because by then I *had* noticed Mama's face. It was so sad, she looked like someone else.

"It's not going to be like that," she said. "When Charlie comes back, we're not going to live together."

I thought she meant he'd go to Warrensburg, but she and I'd still be up here. "He can come to Laglade," I said. My tongue was skipping ahead. "He'll get used to it. And Cody will too, once we're together. That's what counts, for Cody."

"No. That's what counts for *you*, Shana." Mama shook her head slowly. "Cody's accepted the truth. I didn't tell him—he brought it up himself."

"Brought what up?"

She handed me one of those papers, the ones I thought were her test scores. I didn't want to look at it, but she was sitting there watching me, so I had to. The top said *Allen* v. *Allen*.

"What's this?"

"We're getting a divorce." She said it just like that.

"How come?"

"Because I can't go back with him. I thought I could, and I've tried to talk myself into it, but I can't."

"He'll come here," I said again.

"I love Charlie more than anyone, but we can't go on together."

"You have to. You have Cody and me. You can't ruin things for us."

"You'll have to accept it," Mama said.

"I won't!" I stared at her so hard she shrank back, and I guessed that this part—the divorce—was her fault.

"Have you told Daddy?"

"I talked to him before he left for Italy."

I guess she could tell I didn't know. "He flew there last week," she explained.

I couldn't believe it. My face turned red. "He said we'd all go," I mumbled. "He wrote me that."

Mama barely heard. "It's not just the waitress," she said, not looking at me. "I really don't think it is. He said he had to see the Sistine Chapel." Her voice broke then. I felt like tiny shards of glass were falling around me. If I moved or opened my mouth, I'd get cut.

I sat there for a while. She was crying, but I was already so hurt, nothing could make it worse. They had betrayed us, each of them, and there was nothing we could do about it.

Twenty-four

*T*hat night I waited till Mama went to bed, then climbed out the window, carrying the quilt, a flashlight, and the crate with my belongings. A full moon lit my way along the path to the ranger's. I felt drained and empty, like a ghost. I thought I'd known the people I loved best, but one by one—Granddaddy, Daddy, Mama—I'd found pieces that turned them into strangers. Even Cody: *He's accepted the truth*, Mama'd said. I wanted to believe she was lying, but I knew she wouldn't lie about that.

The padlock gleamed on the cabin door. I unlocked it and went in. The room was cold, but there was kindling in the woodbox, so I started a fire in the cast-iron stove. I went out to the woodpile for logs. Moonlight outlined the shed, the pump, the garden. An owl called shrilly, and I thought of the little bluebird, trying to survive against the odds. Was it safe in its birdhouse? Or had it chosen this night, this moon, to fly?

Whooooo . . . The owl's cry echoed from the ridge as I carried wood through the back door. Darkness piled deep in the corners of the room, blotting out the shapes of table and chair, desk and bed. I put two logs in the stove and left the metal door open to help them catch. The flames made shadows on the cabin walls. My foot touched the crate, and I sat down, took out the picture box, and put it in my lap. In the wavering light I sorted the snapshots. Cody's favorites went into the top drawer of the desk; mine I held close, as if they were alive. My fingers traced faces, memories. I ripped them up, one by one, and threw them in the fire.

I cried then, because I knew the family was gone, and nothing would bring it back. Daddy wanted something we didn't have, wanted it so bad he'd crossed the ocean to find it, and Mama was tired of waiting for a man she couldn't count on. I'd dreamed we'd go home together, but it didn't make any difference. Birthday wishes, pennies in the well, the wishbone from Sunday's chicken dinner didn't have magic enough to heal us.

Gram used to read me this nursery rhyme:

> *Humpty Dumpty sat on a wall.*
> *Humpty Dumpty had a great fall.*
> *All the king's horses and all the king's men*
> *Couldn't put Humpty together again.*

"What about Band-Aids? Or glue?" they say I asked. "Shana likes happy endings," Daddy said. "Like me."

But Gram shook her head. She and Granddaddy'd been through hard times too. I guess she knew how fragile some things are, like love and promises and hope.

I went to bed with the quilt wrapped around me. The mattress had the ranger's old-man smell: sweat and woodsmoke and muddy clothes, and I sucked it in, knowing it wouldn't last. When I woke up, dawn had broken to the south. Gray light hung timidly at the front window, like a stranger afraid to knock. I thought of Mama, who would get up and find my empty bed. She'd guess where I was, but she'd have to ask Mrs. Burns for directions. That meant I'd have a few more hours to myself.

I built up the fire in the woodstove and put the kettle on top, to boil water for tea. Then I put my things away: the nature guides upright on the desktop, my knife and flashlight on the kitchen shelf. I copied my poems and stuck them on the wall next to the ranger's maps. My tackle box went by the back door, and the crate next to the bed, with the pretty rocks on top. I tucked the quilt in neatly. Then I washed the big front window, so you could see the river like you were outside.

I decided to go fishing. I headed upstream with the ranger's old fly rod under my arm. I'd found his net hanging on a nail, and I took a bait box and extra hooks. Daddy'd had a fly rod years ago, and he'd showed me how to use it on the Castle. I'd liked the way the thick yellow line hung in midair when you cast it out, and the rod was so limber even bluegills seemed enormous. I passed a rotten log and rolled it over: There were some grubs in the soft, thick bark, and a black beetle. I put them all in the bait box. Mist hung heavy on the river. I passed the flume, with its cascade of water, and dodged through thickets of laurel and rhododendron. After a while I found the pool below the limestone spring. Pale birches overhung the water there, and a shelf of rock offered space to stand and cast. I baited up and looped some line around one hand, then flicked the rod back to put it in the air. It took me a dozen tries to land the grub where the current met still water. Nothing. I reeled in and tried again.

I almost lost track of the time, fishing there; but the mist rose and when I looked upstream there was sunlight winnowing through the tangle of trees and brush. From somewhere on the ridge a sourgum tree cast wine-red leaves on the surface of the river. Something rattled in a thicket up the bank, and I tensed, wondering if some-one was coming. But there was only a deer mouse scut-tling by; leaves drifting on the wind; the murmur of water winding through the gorge.

I changed my bait and decided to try one more cast. The line hung lazy in the air, and I held my breath as the little beetle landed light and easy by a sunken log. Like slow motion a fish rose to the bait. Set the hook! my mind screamed, but I just stood and stared. The ranger used to say you can tell the wild trout by their colors. This one gleamed green and brown, with bright orange spots. It shook its head, and I came to life, snapping the rod back and to the side. The fish jumped again and found spare line to move in, dancing across the pool on its tail. "Wait!" I said out loud, and I grabbed the line and jerked, but there was nothing left but bubbles and a ring of circles and a leader with an empty hook.

Granddaddy said some moments come to us as gifts. I remember walking with him in the field beyond the spring, finding spider webs so hung with dew they looked like silver chains. I wanted to take them home and save them for the Christmas tree, but he said they'd break, so we left them swaying in the tall grass. The memory of the trout was brighter, more alive, but it was also special: one salvageable moment from an awful summer. But standing by that pool, I thought of other moments too: times with the ranger; drifting down the river on my back with Cody; Felix; the cave; a baby slurping milk. I thought of my journal. Gram had used thread to bind what could be saved, but I had words. My quilt would be written: spoken, rhymed, sung, whispered, but also shouted, because anger was a part of it too.

I headed back, pushing through weeds along the riverbank. Mama'd be mad at *me*, I knew. I'd have liked to tell her that my leaving out the window was the last bad thing I'd do; but everything was pared down and turned around. We'd probably fight more. The last two dice on the table, I thought; and I pictured a giant arm sweeping us off in opposite directions.

But maybe, like she'd said, things would get better. I imagined Mama walking from downstream, passing the line of evergreens and seeing the ranger's cabin suddenly, like Cody and I had. She might smile and think: So this is Shana's place. If we were feeling friendly, I'd invite her in; show her my poems; add wood to the stove, so she'd be good and warm after that long walk.

What about Daddy? Would he ever see the ranger's cabin? He'd gone so far away, his face seemed small and faded in my memory, but I spoke to him anyway. *You left us,* I whispered. *You didn't even say good-bye.* He tried to answer but the words were too soft to hear.

Then something pricked my ankle, and I started from my daydream and looked down. My socks were thick with seeds: hitchhikers, sticktights, little brown cockleburrs. I cleared a space on the ground and got down on one knee to pick them off. They clung to the fabric, then to my hands. A tiny drop of blood welled on one finger. It made me think of people I'd lost: Granddaddy, Daddy, Gram, Henry. For some reason I pictured that boy on the school bus, Richie Bird. I brought my hands up close and stared at those burrs. If I ever have a family—my own family—this is how tight I'll hold to them, I thought. I'll cling to them this tight, and never let them go.